DEMONICALLY YOURS

LAUREN PEYTON

Demonically Yours
Book One in the Demon Wars Series
Copyright 2014 Lauren Peyon

Cover Design and Formatting by R.A. Mizer of ShoutLines.
For more information visit Shoutlinesdesign.com.
Cover Image by Kruse Images and Photography
Cover Model: Manny Harvey
Editing by Liz Borino

DEDICATION

I would like to dedicate this to the people who are there for me the most. My family, without whom I would never be able to do any of this. My dear husband, I love you more than you will ever know. I hope you know how much your continued support means to me. You are my own personal knight in shining armor. Finally I would like to dedicate this to my readers, without you guys I wouldn't have anything to write for!

XOXO,

Lauren

finger hovering above his lips. The only sound besides Ava's terrified erratic breaths was his calm, authoritative "Shhh, I need you to be quiet, Ava."

Moments passed slowly as they stood there in the darkness. When she finally calmed enough to be quiet the man pulled his hand away from her face, her eyes wild in panic.

"Who are you?" She reached for the hood that kept his face hidden.

"You are not ready for the truth yet. I need you to be safe. Promise me you will not trust the darkest of us all." The baritone of his voice was soothing to her.

"I am not making any promises to someone I don't know. I haven't even seen your face." She was defiant, strong like everyone said her mother had been.

"It is for your mother," the man said.

"My mother! You knew my mother?" Her mutinous streak shrunk instantly. She missed everything about her mother. She only existed in pictures for her now.

"I loved your mother." The hand that was once around her mouth extended, and as he reached for the top of his hood to pull it from his face, her breath was sucked from her body.

Ava's gasp echoed in the silence. Ava had only seen this man in pictures with her mother. He had been seen and photographed embracing her. Ava's uncle had taken the pictures from her when he caught her looking at them. He was her father.

"Ava, my daughter, I was sentenced to eternity in Hell for my betrayals. Please stay away from the darkest of us all. There is a war coming. You need to be safe. We died for you." The voice sounded weak, as if his time here cost him dearly.

She reached out to touch his face, to feel him. She looked into his eyes and everything was sucked away. The darkness had found her and tore her away.

It was a dream. It was all just a dream. A very screwed up, emotionally damaging, horrible dream. Ava's breath caught in her throat. Her dark hair hung in waves below her shoulders. Somehow she had flung herself up into a sitting position. Her breathing was labored as if she had really just been running for her life. She could feel the hysteria bubbling from her gut. The dream had been vivid. She looked down at her knee, remembering that she had fallen in the damn nightmare, and saw that it was bruised, but she dismissed the injury. She worked at a bar, and she always had unexplainable cuts and bruises.

She climbed out of the queen-size bed she loved. It was warm, and a pillow top, but no matter the comfort level it could not keep her nightmares at bay. They were getting to be more and more frequent. Ava opened the nightstand beside her bed, took out the

Acknowledgements

My wonderful editor Liz, you have been an angel in my mess and sin. Rachel you save me all the time. You ladies are wonderful women and I adore you both.

CHAPTER 1

Running, she was running. Ava's blood umped through her heart as the sting of exertion coursed through her veins. She whipped her head around, but she couldn't see what followed her. Everything around her was shrouded in blackness and wisps of fog. Ava's lungs pounded through her chest. She swore they had their own beat. The sweat began to pool on her forehead. She finally began to recognize where she was. Shapes and figures became more and more clear. Her foot caught on a crumbled headstone and down she went. Her panic rose. She could feel the entity that was following her getting closer. The smell of her own blood permeated the air, tickling her nostrils.

Her foot caught on something. The headstone she had tripped over bore the name of Peter Keznik. She pushed herself up and took off again, trying to keep her pants as silent as she could. Her body wanted to give up, to give into the darkness that was threatening to engulf her. She closed her eyes for a millisecond and oriented herself in the cemetery she had found herself in. Her family's mausoleum where her ancestors were buried was just ahead. Maybe she could hide. Something told her she needed to get there fast. The grass was awash with dew under her bare feet. Her shoes must have gotten lost somewhere in her flight. Ava pumped her legs harder. She was used to running, but this run was spiked with unstoppable fear. One more look behind her and she could see the red orbs in the darkness. A scream threatened to break from her lips.

Ava finally reached the mausoleum and pulled open the door. Silence greeted her. She entered, slamming the portal behind her, and leaned against it in case the evil tried to follow her in. Her labored breaths echoed through the small stone building. She could smell death looming in the air. Her eyes slowly adjusted to the lack of light. She felt in her pocket and grabbed her phone, turning on the flashlight app. Her hands shook as she looked around the enclosed space. What she saw made her screech.

A cloaked figure hovered close to her. As soon as the scream gurgled up from her lips, a hand covered her mouth. The second hand went to the dark hood, one finger hovering above his lips. The only sound besides Ava's terrified erratic breaths was his calm, authoritative "Shhh, I need you to be quiet, Ava."

Moments passed slowly as they stood there in the darkness. When she finally calmed enough to be quiet the man pulled his hand away from her face, her eyes wild in panic.

"Who are you?" She reached for the hood that kept his face hidden.

"You are not ready for the truth yet. I need you to be safe. Promise me you will not trust the darkest of us all." The baritone of his voice was soothing to her.

"I am not making any promises to someone I don't know. I haven't even seen your face." She was defiant, strong like everyone said her mother had been.

"It is for your mother," the man said.

"My mother! You knew my mother?" Her mutinous streak shrunk instantly. She missed everything about her mother. She only existed in pictures for her now.

"I loved your mother." The hand that was once around her mouth extended, and as he reached for the top of his hood to pull it from his face, her breath was sucked from her body.

Ava's gasp echoed in the silence. Ava had only seen this man in pictures with her mother. He had been seen and photographed embracing her. Ava's uncle had taken the pictures from her when he caught her looking at them. He was her father.

"Ava, my daughter, I was sentenced to eternity in Hell for my betrayals. Please stay away from the darkest of us all. There is a war coming. You need to be safe. We died for you." The voice sounded weak, as if his time here cost him dearly.

She reached out to touch his face, to feel him. She looked into his eyes and everything was sucked away. The darkness had found her and tore her away.

It was a dream. It was all just a dream. A very screwed up, emotionally damaging, horrible dream. Ava's breath caught in her throat. Her dark hair hung in waves below her shoulders. Somehow she had flung herself up into a sitting position. Her breathing was labored as if she had really just been running for her life. She could feel the hysteria bubbling from her gut. The dream had been vivid. She looked down at her knee, remembering that she had fallen in the damn nightmare, and saw that it was bruised, but she dismissed the injury. She worked at a bar, and she always had unexplainable cuts and bruises.

She climbed out of the queen-size bed she loved. It was warm, and a pillow top, but no matter the comfort level it could not keep her nightmares at bay. They were getting to be more and more frequent. Ava opened the nightstand beside her bed, took out the leather bound journal and matching pen then started toward the kitchen. She needed tea.

When she turned the light on, the soft hum in the background drew her attention. She hated dead silence. Silence reminded her of the nightmares. She filled the antique kettle her uncle valued. He had told her many stories over tea. He loved to talk about her mother, his youngest sister. She was the most vibrant of them all. She had big plans in life, but had died much too young. That is why Ava intended on living her mother's dreams for her, but her uncle did not think it was the best idea and constantly tried to dissuade her from the impulsivity of the notion. She began to write in her journal. Her pen flew over the paper as she wrote out every detail of her nightmare. She wanted to remember this one, along with many others. It seemed as if they were happening frequently.

The gravelly voice of her Uncle Isaac coming into the kitchen made Ava jump from her seat. "Ava, my miracle. What was your dream about this evening?" he asked gently, and frowned when he saw her frantic movements.

"I had another dream that darkness was coming for me. Uncle, why can't you sleep?" she queried in return. She wanted the attention off herself quickly.

"It is hard to get any sleep when you scream like a beaten cat," he mused. When she was younger and the dreams came, he would burst into her room and cuddle her, but now, he had become accustomed to her screams and woke to have a conversation with her instead of singing her back to sleep with old lullabies in their native tongue.

"I am sorry, Uncle." She stared down at her hands. She noticed her knuckles were white from the stress she felt after tonight's nightmare.

"Tell me about the dream, child." He sat beside her in the bright kitchen.

"It was about some man. I think he's my father. Some evil was trying to get me, and I found him." She explained the gist of the dream.

"I see. Perhaps I should find you a dream catcher, or a pendant to protect you from the evil eye." His age and wise nature shone through his words and tone.

"It isn't necessary. I'll try to clear the thoughts myself; mind over matter." She stood as the kettle whistled to gain attention.

As she was preparing cups for them both, he spoke again. "I would still feel better if you wore something to protect yourself from the evil eye. Please, indulge an old man."

She looked at her uncle. He was the closest thing to a father she had ever known. After her mother died, she had no one to turn to but him. He raised Ava and treated her like she was his own child and not just his niece. That is why she still lived with him. She loved him. Ava carried the full cups over to the table and placed one in front of him, testing her own out after adding honey and stirring. "I will, if that is what you wish."

He nodded and sipped his tea. He liked it plain. Isaac didn't care for putting in every fancy additive you could find. Tea was meant to be a certain way. He believed that, and never faltered from his traditional styling. He was one of the few remaining members of the family. It was mainly just Ava and Uncle, as she called him. His hand found hers and tapped it in a loving motion. "Enjoy your tea. I will find you what I think will help you tomorrow, while you are in classes. Perhaps, your dream is about your job?"

"Not this conversation again," she groaned audibly.

"Ava, your job is not suitable for a young woman of your nature," he spoke calmly.

"It is suitable, for now. I like my job. It is fun."

"You could have fun at the antique shop, little lovely." He used the affectionate term like a weapon.

"If I lose my job, I will come and work for you," she leveled with him.

"All I ask is that you are safe. You are all I have, Ava."

They both knew the truth. Ava *was* all he had, and he was all Ava had. They had friends, acquaintances, but nothing close like they were. Ava had tried dating, but she could never place her trust in any man besides her uncle for a long time. After the cups of tea were finished, Ava stood, returning to the stove and kettle. "Do you want any more tea?"

"No, we both need rest. I trust you will go back to bed and not be on your cell phone all night? You need to be on time for your classes tomorrow." He scolded. He knew about the younger generation's obsession with cell phones, and, in particular, hers.

"Yes, Uncle," she placated him with her soft smile.

Ava rinsed the kettle and cleaned the cups while her uncle walked back to his room. When she was finished, she walked back to her bedroom and looked around. It was clean, not a shred of fiber out of place. She shook her head at her own thoughts. Ava knew her dream was crazy. Her father would not try to contact her. He had left her mother while she was pregnant. As far as Ava knew, he was dead, too. She didn't care much about the fact that she didn't know him. There was a part of her, however, that wanted to meet him. Ava crawled into bed and turned off her side-table light. Her uncle was right. She did have class the next day and needed the sleep.

The alarm clock sounded early. Ava smacked it into silence and went into the bathroom to get ready for school. She showered slowly to let the heat of the water sink into her muscles. The past night's dream had taken a toll on her. She was thankful when she didn't dream again after she went back to bed. She had slept the peaceful sleep of the dead. She washed her mahogany locks with her favorite shampoo. The scent tickled her nose. Once she was finished with her morning ritual, she wrapped her hair into a towel so she could dry the rest of her body off. She was far from perfect in her own eyes.

She could stand to lose a few pounds. They were just stubborn and didn't want to be lost. Her legs were long and looked great in a skirt, but she still felt insecure at times about most of her body. Ava wasn't obese and many people wished they had her looks, but she knew in reality they didn't, she was different from them and they knew it. She was dangerous because she was different. Ava believed that some sort of birth defect she suffered caused her eyes to be a vivid shade of violet, what the defect was Isaac never explained to her, to him she was beautiful and one of a kind. Sometimes the color faded to a darker purple, but most of the time, her eyes were the bright color that was shining back at her from the mirror at this very moment.

While her hair dried, she applied her makeup. She played up her pouty lips, so the focus would be drawn off her eyes. She leaned over the sink and lined her lips in an almost cherry red color. She smiled and thought of the outfit she would wear. Ava kept working on her lips till they were perfectly colored and glossed. The rest of her makeup was light and casual. Even her own gaze was drawn away from her eyes to her lips in the mirror. Her smile spread. Next, was her hair, which was long and swayed to the middle of her back; so thick and full with natural highlights. She could see where her mother shone through in her looks. The unfamiliar pieces of her face, she attributed to her father.

It took a while for her hair to blow dry once she took the hair dryer out to continue her routine. Wisps of hair flowed around her face. She let them fly around. She was impressed at how quick her look was coming together. She exited her bathroom only to hear her phone chirping that she had a message.

Ava pulled on her favorite black lace, boy shorts panties and a matching bra. Pulling on a tight pair of light wash denim jeans, after she was dressed she went to her phone the message was from her friend, Michael. They met during English, and now also had Business class together.

"Ava, don't forget our meeting in the student lounge."

She laughed. He really knew she could be a space cadet, especially since her nightmares had gotten worse. She texted back quickly.

"Yes, I remember. See you there."

Ava hit send and put her phone back on the charger. She went to her closet to find her black shirt. It clung to her frame wonderfully. The black fabric was an off-the-shoulder piece that showed off her collarbone. The dark black really offset the soft tan tone of her skin. Ava went back to the bathroom to look herself over. After brushing her teeth and spraying herself with her favorite perfume, she inhaled and smiled. Ava felt the perfume was perfect for her.

Her walk to the kitchen didn't take long. She found her uncle eating his breakfast, dry toast with eggs. The sound of his fork scraping the plate made Ava shake her head.

"Uncle, I'm leaving for school. I'll be home this evening for a while before work," she announced.

"Good, I'll be at the shop, but I should be around for dinner if you want to eat before your shift." His smile warmed her heart.

"That sounds like a date." She beamed at him.

"I will see you this evening. Now, go. The traffic is bad this morning. Worse than usual, I mean," he joked.

"Yes, Uncle." She grabbed her keys off of the wall hanger and went out to her little car to start it. Ava loved her car 2010 Honda Civic. It was amazing on gas, and a stunning red. Of course, she had a few speeding tickets she never told her uncle about, but she paid them and was more cautious of how fast she went. She took off toward the university to start the long day of classes.

She pulled into the parking lot and parked in her favorite lot. She was lucky enough to get first row parking. Sometimes people had fought over the lack of parking at this place. Ava herself had been late to class more than one time in order to find parking near the campus without risking a tow. She ran into the student lounge and looked for Michael. Her phone chimed once more, the alarm to head to class was going off. The meeting would have to wait for the hour between classes. She quickly paid for a bottle of water, and an apple then ran for class.

Ava barely got to the doors before the professor locked them. He was a strict teacher, but he was good. She had already taken almost a whole notebook full of notes just in his class. She saw Michael wave at her from his normal seat. Ava went toward him to take her own. She was glad he knew enough not to be late waiting on her. After a brief hello back and forth with Michael, she got out her notebook as the professor started his lecture.

He was around six feet tall. He wore argyle almost every day. He reminded Ava of her uncle. The way he spoke was authoritative and no nonsense. Ava took detailed notes about the assignment. They were to work together to create an outline and actual project on the science behind business. It was a heavy project. There would be check-ins about the project and the students would work in groups and needed to show progress at each check-in. After getting all of the details about what would be acceptable, Professor Von James dismissed the class.

Michael and Ava walked out, talking already about the class period. It had ended early, which was great for them. It was time for coffee. They took seats in the red lounge chairs after the female barista served them. Ava smiled at her companion. They were prattling about different ideas that had already come to them.

"What about a Power Point?" he asked.

"No, I bet most of the class will be doing that. I want something memorable, something to get an A with," she countered.

"Okay. Well, we can do a Power Point and something else to go with it. That way, we can print out the slides as handouts so people can keep up with our project." He was good at these things.

"All right, we can do that. But I want visuals, handouts, the PowerPoint, and a mock up of what we are proposing." She knew she sounded anal about this, but it was her future in jeopardy she could not afford an error that she could have prevented by simply editing.

"You are a grade Nazi, aren't you?"

"Yes, how could you tell?"

"Oh, just some air about you told me."

"So, you can do the PowerPoint, since you are the guru on those. I can start drafting a proposal…" They were working hard on this one.

Ava inhaled the smell of the coffee. It was almost as comforting to her, as the tea was in the wee hours of this morning. They worked quickly, and before long, they had the entire project roughly outlined. Ava was ready to start the research and collect what she needed for their project. *We'll be getting an A for sure,* she thought.

When the coffee cups were drained and they were running out of steam, Ava stood. "I should go. I have another class in…" She looked at her cell phone to find the time and gasped, "I can't believe we worked right through it. Shit."

"Are you kidding me?"

"No joke, we worked right through our classes."

"Do you have to go?"

"Yes, I do. I have a very important meeting I can't miss." She meant her uncle.

Ava stood from their comfortable spot and hugged Michael. She packed up her belongings and waved as she walking away from the lounge area. She hitched her messenger bag onto her side and took off toward the parking lot. She was having a conversation in her head about what had happened today. She spent hours with Michael. He was a handsome devil; a tall, dark, handsome devil. She laughed at his Michael's flirtatious ways and didn't see what was coming her way.

She opened the door to leave the main hall and hit something hard. Ava fell hard on her backside. Her eyes wandered up and saw someone tall and built like a Greek God. The sun was filtering in behind the brick wall of a human she had just run into. She could see his olive toned skin and hair that was as black as night. The stranger extended his hand extended toward her. She took it as he began to speak. "I'm sorry I knocked you over, miss. Are you all right?" The man's voice was smooth and low; and very pleasing to the ears.

"Yes, I am okay." She tried her best not to stammer or drool. Ava's brain had already started a chant about how it isn't cool to drool.

The guy pulled her upright. "Are you sure you don't need an escort to your car?"

"No, I'm fine," she reassured him, she couldn't place the accent he had. Perhaps it was one of the European accents.

"I'm Chris," the man said easily.

"Ava, nice to meet you." She remembered some semblance of her manners at this point.

"Ava, that is a pretty name. I hope I run into you again at some point." His chest rumbled, was he laughing?

"Yeah, with less hitting my ass on the ground." Her hand ran over her sore cheeks.

"If you aren't too busy plowing ahead like a train on a track." His smirk made her jaw drop. It was obvious to him that she found him attractive.

"Sure, I'll see you around, Chris." She managed not to stutter.

"That sounds nice. You sure you don't want me to walk you to your car?" Chris seemed to care, but she didn't trust him.

"No thank you. I'm sure I can manage." Ava tried her own smile on him.

"I'll see you soon, Ava." He inclined his head and walked off into the lounge

She was dumbfounded. Her eyes raked over Chris as he walked off then shook her head, trying to clear it. She was going to have tea with her uncle. She needed her head clear because he was shrewd. Her uncle would see anything like lust in her eyes and give her a lecture about it.

Ava's breath returned to normal and she took off for her car to hurry home. She still wanted to get a nap in before dinner and work. The time dwindled down faster and faster with each moment she wasted. Sure, Chris was hot, but she knew nothing about him. For all she knew, he was a player just like she imagined her father to be. As her thoughts wandered, they became darker. Why was he so interested in her? Why did he want to walk her to her car so bad? Shivers cascaded down her spine. Ava decided that tomorrow she would be parking in a different spot to make sure she wasn't followed. She slipped into her car quickly and drove home to salvage what time she could.

Caine knew his target, her scent was vague, but he was still able to trace her. When she pulled into the parking lot, he cloaked himself in the darkness surrounding the university. He prowled alongside her, watching her walk. Her dark hair pulled back, accentuating her collarbone and the tan of her flesh. Caine bared his teeth with a barely audible growl. She was attractive, but this was a recruit. He had to bring her over to their side. The war was just erupting in Hell. The factions were uneasy and there was more violence than normal in the pits.

He came back to his current task, which was to watch this young woman; watch over her and protect her until she was ready to know the truth about her heritage… her life. The facts about what happened to her father were horrible. Why he was condemned to be a prisoner of the pit was unimaginable. Caine knew about Avaraz's demise. He was one of the search party heads who came for Avaraz in the end. Caine edged closer and closer, almost emerging from his hiding spot, the scent of her getting stronger in his nose. She was a half-breed. There was no mistaking that from so close.

Caine watched as she walked into the college. She went straight to the lounge as if she was looking for someone, her eyes adjusted slowly to the different lighting in the lounge, after a few moments she took out her phone and then ran. She must have been late. Caine laughed. The silly girl had no clue what demon bait she was. His eyes closed and he began to follow her through the eyes of the sinners around. They were numerous and some of these humans were very entertaining in their sins. It was easy for him to keep tabs on her. He was of the warrior-class of demons. He had lived through wars before. He had survived the worst tortures and pains one could imagine, but rarely had he accessed this part of his powers. The professor who droned on to the class couldn't have been duller. His voice was a flat monotone. Caine almost fell asleep while he waited for the lecture to end.

He waited. Caine waited for hours more. From his previous trips from hell to watch her, he knew she had other classes she would be attending. But for some reason, she went back to the lounge and began to speak to someone. Caine's curiosity was peaked. He watched and listened into the conversation. They were planning the project the professor had outlined in class. No wonder he felt as if he were about to fall asleep.

He drew his hand through his black hair. He could feel the red in his eyes glow. A demon's nature was to collect the souls of the sinners and make deals. The college was full of sins just itching to be plucked. There were souls waiting for deals to be made. Caine's teeth ground with the control he had to exhibit here. His mission was not to collect souls, right now. His mission was to recruit the new half-breed and bring to light her special heritage. Her father had entrusted him with her name. Now, Caine was collecting details about her life, trying to figure out which way would be easiest for him to gain her trust and get her to believe him. He didn't have time to fail.

Finally, he watched the girl check her phone. What was the deal with that electronic device? It was like her master, chiming at her and demanding attention. She started loading her bag up and Caine knew this was his moment. He came from the shadows and adjusted his eyes. The demonic red would scare the female. She would have a hard enough time trusting him without the instant shock of his red eyes set into his olive skin.

She was moving like a speeding train. Her mind was completely lost and a snarl of one thought after the other. One thought was predominant, tea. She was planning to go have tea with her uncle. How fitting. She may need the tea after this encounter. He reached to open the door and she plowed into his chest. Even though it was against his nature he didn't stop her fall or reach to grab her. He was pretending to be normal. It wasn't time yet.

He spoke to her, using his most soothing tone. "I am sorry I knocked you over, miss. Are you all right?"

By the time she was back on her feet and prepared to leave, he could tell she was aroused. The way her breath hitched in her throat was a physical reaction to his proximity. Her violet eyes, the symbol of a half-breed, were on him. He could feel her taking in each part of his body, and he may have flexed. He had lied about his name. He said it was Chris, but again, only to protect them both. She wasn't ready to know the truth about him or her true nature and this certainly was not the correct time or place to reveal such a thing as her lineage to her. When he helped her up, he slipped a small piece of fabric from her bag. He wasn't sure what it was until she walked away. He could see her slight shudder. She shook her head. Caine kept his distance and didn't follow her. His brief contact with her would awaken more of her demon side. He needed to get back to the pit before anyone became curious about what he was doing. The war was still bubbling and factions were breaking off.

Caine forced magic from his body. The cool air of the New York City autumn fell away as he shimmered back to hell. The hot flames licked at his body. He dropped the brown-eyed glamour trick he used on earth. He took the small memento of his meeting out of his pocket. It was a scarf, and it was saturated in her scent. He would be able to track her anywhere now, which he may need to do.

He walked past the screaming souls, the trapped ones, the damned ones. They begged for forgiveness, but it would never come for them. This area of hell was reserved for the ones who denied the Almighty. They denied God and refused to repent, even when the Angel of Death had his fingers wrapped around their neck. Caine stuffed the scarf back into his pocket and went in search of where Avaraz was being held. The prisoner was chained to one of the many walls that surrounded the circles of Hell. Each circle of hell was protected, each sin separated. Many people knew of the seven deadly sins, but most didn't understand exactly how deadly they were.

Caine dealt with the sin of lust, and he was built to be lusted after. Many women had fallen prey to his predatory nature. He bedded many of them without a second thought and never felt a thrill before or after his conquests. He took many souls for his faction. Lust was a many splendored thing. People lusted for money, food, fame, power, or sex. Each petty desire a person had could lead to them making a deal for their soul.

The prisoner was held by the souls he had collected for the walls. Avaraz was slunk down passed out. The hold of the chains drained his powers to keep him weak, the souls ate away at his being. The process was painful. Avaraz was here because of his decisions with Ava's mother. When he was ordered to New York City by the devil himself to prevent a woman from becoming a guardian angel. When Avaraz was in his prime his job was assassin. He was a demon for the record books. He was able to seduce angels to the dark side. His tantric tongue worked wonders for them. Stealing the souls from more than willing victims.

Avaraz had been around for thousands of years. Since the beginning, he watched the rise and fall of many factions. He had contributed to lust being the favorite sin of the devil for many years, but since his indiscretion lust had never been chosen again. Caine remembered the day Avaraz was sent to Christina. He had spent days out of hell, then weeks away became, months. Finally, the devil summoned his demon. Avaraz reported his progress, but lied to the Elders. The dark prince let Avaraz go, but sent a throng of demons to follow him. When his lies caught up with him, Caine was sent after his one-time comrade in arms.

Caine shook the memories from his head and approached the wall Avaraz was attached to. "Wake up, Avaraz."

Blazing red eyes blinked up at him, slowly coming to consciousness. "Did you find her?"

"Yes, my quest was successful, my friend." Caine used the term loosely. Demons didn't band together normally on a level beyond the battlefield. Demons did not make friends or play nice.

"Does she look like her mother?" The traces of his original accent were plain in his voice, as was the exhaustion that was echoed in the hollows of his face.

"She looks like her mother, aye, but the child bears a resemblance to you, as well." Caine spoke in measured words.

"I wish I could look upon her just once and have her see me." Avaraz's whisper was pained.

"Do you feel her at all?" Caine asked.

"Yes, I feel her sometimes. I have been able to project into her dreams a few times, but it has drained me more, I fear. I will soon lose everything." His sage-like voice stopped after his realization.

"I will watch for her. There is a strong aura around her. Perhaps, bringing her into the war will be what is needed for us to regain glory with the prince," Caine suggested.

"She is not ready. She doesn't even know me, let alone of our existence." Avaraz sounded fierce in his conviction.

"As you wish. Perhaps this will make you feel her more." Caine retrieved the scarf from his pocket and dangled it around Avaraz's face. The instant it was before him, Avaraz took a large inhale to memorize her scent and be able to connect to her.

"She smells like her mother. I gave her mother that scarf. Christine wore it the day I chose her to be mine, and she chose me as hers." It was rare, but some demons did still have enough of a heart to love.

"I see." Caine took another smell of the fabric, memorizing the sweet honeysuckle scent wafting off it.

"Protect her," Avaraz pleaded.

"I will do my best, but the war is escalating. They may even let you off the wall in order to have more soldiers," he stated.

"No, they will never let me go for my lies to the prince. I need you to protect my daughter," again his friend pleaded with him.

"I will try. But if she threatens us, I will be forced to give her scent to the hunters and she will come here for her training." Caine knew this was not what Avaraz wanted to hear, but it was the truth.

"I understand, but train her there. Her uncle knows of us and has never spoken a word. He protects Ava for Christina, and for me. The house they live in is sealed by magic. Demons would not sense the presence. It cost me dearly." It would cost Avaraz more in the end.

"If she will trust me, I will," Caine promised once again.

"Thank you, my friend." Avaraz closed his eyes. The wall was slowly draining him, it sucked out just enough energy to keep him weakened and unable to break the spell, yet kept him alive to feel the pain and the years pass.

Caine bowed his head. "Farewell, my friend. I will return with news of your daughter shortly."

There was not another sound coming from the other demon. Caine shimmered away from the area. His body content with the heat in this section of hell, he appeared back in his quarters. There were sounds of death, fighting, and demon on demon devastation. The war was only beginning and the Collectors were already out, searching for the weaklings of the race. Caine had to plan his next steps carefully. He needed to get to Ava before it was too late.

CHAPTER 2

Michael screamed as the flames engulfed him. Smoke shrouded the handsome features of his face. His voice thundered with pure agony. His brown eyes filled with tears. He was reaching for Ava. Her fear kept her from reaching back, while the scene before her intensified. She could feel the heat against her face as the fire roared behind Michael.

"MICHAEL!" she screamed for him.

He was unable to speak at all. There was a flame covering his mouth. The only sound was a muffled scream and the crackling of the fire. Ava was full of fear. A dark cloud barreled toward him. Ava put her hands out to brace herself from the darkness that threatened to encircle her.

Her hands lit up with what looked like electricity, pure energy. She could feel it balling in her hand. Before she knew what to do, a ball with bolts leading out flew from her hand. It looked like her hand was the night sky during a lightning storm. She screamed, afraid of what just happened.

Ava flew out of bed, her body covered in sweat. Another dream; this dream felt so real. Tears clouded her eyes. She wondered if she was going insane. She picked up her phone and sent a text to Michael.

I had a bad dream. Are you okay? -Ava

Thankfully, he responded before she even had time to get out of her bed.

Yes, I am fine. It must have been a vivid dream if you had to text me. Want to talk? —M

It's fine. Just wanted to know you were okay. I'll see you in class. —Ava

She tossed her phone back on her side-table and stretched.

"Uncle?" she asked when she entered the hall.

"In the kitchen, our tea is ready," he answered.

Ava entered the kitchen and grinned at her uncle. She had a brief flash of the man from earlier and her body flushed. Ava pushed the thought away. She took her seat next to her uncle as he prepared her cup.

"Are you well, my niece?" He asked once she was settled.

"Yes, I'm okay. I did have another dream, though."

"I heard your scream. Was it more frightening than usual? Do you want to tell me about it?"

"Just realistic. I even woke up sweating." She tried to laugh.

Concern crossed his face. He quickly tried to change the subject, obviously uncomfortable. "Do you have work tonight?"

"Yes, I do, Uncle. I am going to need to get ready soon. Are you going back to the shop tonight?"

"Yes, I have meetings tonight. I will probably not return till about ten or eleven tonight." His eyes closed and he took a sip of his tea.

"I'll come see you before I leave, Uncle. I love you." She kissed his forehead then left the table to head back to her room.

Ava worked at a bar near campus. It was the hangout for most of the college students. She knew many of the faces. It did not mean it was her favorite place to work. She toyed with the black corset she wore. It had silver buckles on it, and her jean skirt covered just enough to keep things interesting.

She slipped on her black boots and went from her bedroom to the bathroom. Her hair was still braided from earlier in the day, so she took the braid out, her fingers working deftly. Her thick mahogany hair flowed free in beach waves. Ava finger-combed her hair and sprayed it into place then started on her makeup. She accented her lips again and lined her eyes. She didn't place too much emphasis on her makeup for work. The night would include drinks spilled on her, cleaning up messes, and getting sweaty. Why on earth would she want to get gussied up, just to get messy?

The night was rough. It was a Monday and that meant it would be slow. She was forced to do the most mundane tasks because no one in the bar liked to do them between waiting on the few customers who dribbled in during the early part of her shift. She restocked all the fruit and refilled all the juices. She would also have to check the fountain drinks. Once everything was perfect in her area, she took her first break. She grabbed her phone and saw several texts.

Haven't heard back from you. Are you good? —M

You're starting to worry me. —M

Did you lose your phone? —M

Kidnapped? —M

I'm going to stalk you till you respond (joke). —M

Ava had to laugh. She was the one who was having the horrible dreams where he was being burned for some reason, yet he was worried about her because she had a bad dream. She finally sent him a message in return.

I'm fine. Sorry I didn't respond earlier. I have been at work. Slow night so far. I'll see you in class tomorrow. —Ava

She closed the phone and Ava put her feet up on another chair in the back room. Her eyes soon closed. She started thinking about the guy she ran into. Chris was huge, easily six feet six inches and three hundred pounds of pure muscle. His gorgeous black hair curling at the edges was thick. She wondered what it would be like to run her hands through it. Out of reflex, she ran her fingers through her own hair.

Too soon, it was time for her to go back to work. When she resumed her post behind the bar, she wiped the wet cloth over a few spots patrons had left and collected the tips they left her in return. Ava's boss soon came up behind her and tapped her ass.

"Damn it, Dom," she blurted.

"Well, it was mine for a bit," he joked

"Sexual harassment," she bit back.

"Okay, okay. Sorry. You do have a nice ass, though. What do you think about cutting out early? I have to save some labor hours and you got all the side work done already." His green eyes danced.

"Sure, I guess I can. I was getting bored, anyways." She put down the cloth and took off her pouch.

"Sweet. Thank you, beautiful." Dom pulled her into a hug and kissed the top of her head. Their romance had been brief and private, but hot.

Ava still had a hard time resisting the charms of the man who was her boss. He had brown hair, but eyes the color of emeralds. He was unbelievable in bed. Ava thought back over their short-lived time together with fondness. They were friends now, and worked closely most shifts, even if he did get hands-on at times. She closed out her till then clocked out.

"All right, I'm heading out." She announced to Dom.

"Thanks, beautiful. I owe you one." He winked.

"You owe me more than one. See you soon." She chuckled and walked away.

"I hope you'll hold me to it," he yelled out so she could hear it.

She walked out the back door laughing. He was a hound, but an entertaining hound. Ava started her trek home. The area was not known for good parking. Along the way, she passed by her uncle's shop. Ava decided to stop in to visit. She opened the door and the bells jingled.

"Hello?" she ventured.

"In the back, my dear," Ava's uncle would recognize her voice anywhere, just as she did his.

Ava followed around the back of the counter and found her uncle with paper in his hands. "Uncle, what are you reading?" He rarely had his hands around something that wasn't printed type, but this was something hand written.

"What is that, Uncle?" she questioned him.

"You, my love, do not need to be interested in this matter."

He began to close the letter; Ava's eyes scanned the paper.

"Is that a letter from my mother?" Ava knew her mother was gone, but she still craved every piece of her mother she could get her hands on.

"Yes, your mother knew her death was impending and she wrote this note for me." He tucked the folded paper into his coat pocket.

"Can I see it?" She pressed him. Her uncle did not keep secrets from her normally.

"No, my darling, you cannot. You are not ready for this letter and I must keep you safe from certain things a while longer. Please do not press. When you are ready I will share this. I promise," he attempted to comfort her.

"I understand. I just miss her."

Ava had lost her mother when she was young, too young to remember most things. The only memories she had were of her mom's scent, and the videos they saved. Her father had not appeared in any of them, but Christina was always happy. Ava had a series of letters her mother had written for her before she started her slope toward death.

"Ava, you are the spitting image of your mother. I have tried to give you every piece of her I could. I have even gotten family videos from the old country. You have more than some people ever will. I want you to be patient," he warned her.

"I will."

Her uncle knew how stubborn, inquisitive, and how determined she was. Ava had already thought of ways to find the letter and read it, but he stopped that. This was a serious issue judging by his tone. He rarely used it. She only remembered him using this tone when it concerned her safety.

"Are you ready to go, Uncle?" she continued the conversation, "I am happy for our nightcap."

"Yes, I have concluded my business for tonight." He sounded weary.

"Do you want to stop at our favorite place for dinner? It's on the way home if we walk," she suggested.

"Absolutely not. We will not be *walking* anywhere. A lady walking the streets at night in New York City is inappropriate without a stronger male escort." He burst out.

"You are a strong male, Uncle," she tried to placate him.

"Not strong enough. I am an older man. If you had a younger man who would scare the miscreants of this city, I would be more amenable, but not this time. Not right now. The world is too dangerous, my dearest treasure." Isaac had to explain to her. His worry was paramount.

Isaac's life had been dedicated to protecting her from something, from whatever stole her mother. Ava did not understand why he was so protective, but he was. Isaac said there was some sort of accident caused by the medical team in the hospital after her mother got sick. There was nothing anyone could do to stop it, but he wanted to protect her from the same heartbreak her mother experienced during her dying days. Again, Ava did not understand completely what her uncle meant. Sometimes, fate had a different plan. Her uncle had to understand if death wanted her early as it did her mother, he couldn't stop it.

Some things were inevitable.

The war was coming fast. Caine's skin felt tight. Another demon was lost during his time with Avaraz. Caine had come back to the council chambers for the Lust demons and found them all abuzz with the newest information.

"What happened?" he demanded. Caine was a soldier. He did as he was told and lusted for his time in battle. He relished the fight.

Avaraz's words still echoed in Caine's head. The wish of a demon much older than him was almost undeniable. With all the demons dying on earth, Caine gave more thought to fulfilling his promise to Avaraz. Protecting the girl would prove simple. Her scent wasn't strong. A demon hunter wouldn't suspect her. The eyes were the only otherworldly things about her. She was an ordinary human otherwise. His scouting mission proved useful for that, at least.

"More attacks, three dead. Bastion's safe-house was compromised. We need to move everyone."

"Where? If we're being hunted, we're being watched. If we move them, it puts another safe house at risk." One of the elders growled and banged his meaty fist against the table.

Looking around the table, Caine spoke when things calmed down. "Vladimir, I agree we risk more exposure if we move them. We need to collect our forces. If this is a war between the hunters and the demons, we need to put up a strong front. Call together the councils, and call all the factions together."

"All the factions?" several voices spoke at once asking the same questions.

"Yes, all the factions. The hunters are not normal. If they are finding and killing us already, then we need power and we need to attack. The last war between the hunters and us nearly decimated an entire sin."

"Why should we care what happens to the other sins?" One of the younger demons spoke up with an insolent tone.

"We are demons. All of us have a stake in the war." Caine rose from his chair, crossed the room, and picked up the other demon by his throat. "If one of us dies, the entire balance is thrown off, and the war between demons will start again."

A snarl escaped from the other demon. Fire flashed in Caine's eyes.

"We need to convene the elders." He spoke succinctly once more and dropped the younger man into his chair.

"As you wish," the lesser demon submitted to the elder.

Caine was ready to lead the warriors into battle.

Saturday was another day of work for Ava. She donned her usual work clothing, dark and sexy. She was in the locker room when Tonya walked in. Tonya and Ava had no love lost. Ava had Dom in her back pocket, and Tonya wanted him. She hated Ava had been with the man and he was stuck on her still. The two didn't acknowledge each other. Ava finished putting her items away and turned to walk out. Tonya moved her shoulder into Ava's with force and made Ava stumble. She had to fight to catch her balance.

"What the hell?" she bit out.

"Go to hell, skank." Tonya rolled her eyes, but there was a light in them that let Ava know the woman was pleased with herself.

"Excuse me?" Ava crossed her arms.

"You heard me. Go suck dick." Tonya dropped her bag and stood toe to toe with Ava.

"Are you still jealous because I had something you will never have?" Ava taunted.

"Like I said, go to hell." Tonya tried to make herself taller.

"Nice comeback, you vapid cow!" Ava shot back.

No more words were exchanged. Tonya's hand pulled back and started toward Ava's head. In pure instinct and adrenaline, Ava ducked her head and everything moved in slow motion, Tonya's hand smashed into a locker and Ava countered with an elbow blow to Tonya's ribcage. When Tonya bent over to collect air back into her lungs Ava landed one more blow to the other woman's back.

Tonya went to her knees and howled in pain. The door burst open and Dom's green eyes went wide. "Shit, Loca! What did you do?"

Ava's chest heaved. "The bitch started it. I finished it."

"I need you to go home now."

"She started insulting me and when she attacked, I countered."

Ava could swear she was literally seeing red. The violence in the encounter was almost a relief. It had been a long time coming. While the dislike between the two women was not a secret, Ava had never acted on it before. She was usually so self-controlled. Ava flexed her hands then grabbed her bag and walked out. When the cold air outside hit her lungs, she took a deep breath. She didn't realize her body was running so hot at the time.

Ava took off toward her Uncle's home, her home. He was the only father she knew. When she got home she called out for her Isaac.

"Uncle," her singsong filled the air.

There was no response. She walked into the kitchen where he usually poured over random documents. He wasn't there. She found a note on the fridge in Isaac's familiar handwriting:

Ava, my darling niece,

I had business to tend to at the shop. Please forgive my absence. I shall prepare dinner once I am finished with the work I need to do. I love you to the moon and stars.

Uncle

Ava read the note. Uncle loved his shop. He would live there if he didn't have to tend to her as he felt he should. She scrawled out a reply:

Uncle Isaac-

If you get home before me, please call my cell phone. I am going to work on a school project with Michael, my lab partner. I love you to the sun and back.

Ava

She laughed thinking about their endearments. She called Michael next.

"Hello, handsome."

"Hey, beautiful."

"Mind if I come over?"

"For what?" He sounded almost hopeful.

"To have you impregnate me," she said without missing a beat.

"Wh-What?" he sputtered.

Ava had to bite her lip to keep from slipping into a giggle fit. "Michael, we have that project we need to work on. That's why I want to come over."

"Okay, I'll see you soon." He sounded like he had gotten up to start cleaning judging by the amount of background noise that had started.

"See you." Dropping her phone back in her bag, she turned to leave.

When she arrived at Michael's brownstone, Ava took the stairs slowly. She was never a fan of them at the gym and certainly wouldn't make them a favorite here, either. He opened the door after two quick raps of her fist. Michael was waiting for her, how sweet… or was that creepy? Ava never really had much success with dating. The longest relationship she had ever had was with her manager and that wasn't exactly an ethical relationship.

"Took you long enough," he bantered quickly. A boyish smile on his face warmed her quickly.

"I had to make sure I had the right gloss." She rolled her eyes and set her bag down. "I thought we could start with outlines and sources tonight."

"Aye, aye, captain" He gave a salute.

"Stop that." Ava giggled and then wanted to kick herself in the ass because the last thing she needed right now was to give Michael hope that she liked him as more than a lab partner.

"You should laugh more often," Michael's eyes seemed to glow looking at her, "are you hungry?"

"No, sorry, I made plans for dinner." She kept the "with my uncle" silent. Maybe if he thought she had a boyfriend, it would be easier for him.

"With who?" he questioned as he opened his laptop his interest was blatantly obvious.

"Isaac, my uncle," she explained. Obviously he was good at twenty-questions, so the faster she divulged, the sooner they could get to work.

"I see…"

Three hours, later Ava still hadn't gotten a call. The duo had outlined their entire project, and made detailed starting notes with annotated bibliographies for each source, which they could refer to later. It would all go into a heavy package for their professor.

"I better go. It's getting late." She stood to stretch her limbs.

"Want a ride? I got my Ducati." His brows waggled.

"Are you kidding? If my uncle knew I got on one of those, he'd skin me alive, then filet you." She laughed.

"I can take it." He winked at her.

"I'll walk. My uncle's shop isn't far, so I'll just walk there."

"You sure?"

"Yes, I can handle myself."

"All right, then." He walked her to the door and stood, as if he were waiting to kiss her.

Ava ducked under his arm to keep him from pulling her close. She could feel the dismay roll off him in waves. She was good with sensing others' emotions. She always could, since she was a child. She was an empathic individual.

"I'll see you in class," she offered as a farewell and started down the stairs.

She made it outside before taking a deep breath and relaxing. Michael was cute. He would be a good man to date, but something just wasn't right with him. Ava didn't feel the heat she desired. She pulled her jacket tighter around her thin frame and started walking toward the shop.

Several blocks away, Isaac was doing paperwork. His psychic had left him with many questions. He had to take out the letter and read it twice more. It was a letter his sister left before her tragic death many years ago. He had a weekly appointment with the psychic woman. Ava didn't know the psychic came, even though Ava was normally the topic of his desires to know the future. The cards read only of troubles, sorrow, and death. She pulled them twice with the same result.

Even though the psychic tried to explain to Isaac that the cards might not exactly mean what they read, he knew better. There was always death on the horizon for Ava. His niece was the center of his world. He had taken so many steps to prevent it, but his efforts seemed futile, especially when Caine entered his shop.

"What are you doing here?" Isaac was at his front counter in seconds, ready to defend till his last breath.

"I am well. Yes, I will take coffee, my friend," Caine answered.

"You are not welcome here, demon." Isaac was firm.

"Like it or not, I am the only one who can help Ava." Caine closed the distance.

"She will not be like you. She has a soul," Isaac bit, feisty as ever.

"And I have many. She does not have a choice. You cannot protect her with little spells. I found her by scent alone, which means her powers are growing. She will become more like me, and sooner than you would ever guess." Caine was cold, accessing every desire the man ever had.

"You lust for the psychic you saw tonight. Give me access to Ava now, and I will give the psychic to you." Caine loved the look he received.

"That is none of your concern, and I will not sell my soul nor my niece's soul for your falsehoods."

"Would you rather see your darling Ava dead?" Caine interrupted.

"What?"

"That got your attention. There are demon hunters. We are being hunted to near extinction and the hunters do not care if one is quarter, half, or full. If you have demonic blood in you then you are a target for assassination. Four nests have now been hit and destroyed. Our Collectors have not even been able to find a scrap of their souls. Do you want Ava to live?"

"Of course I want her to live." Isaac was trying to lower his voice. The concern he felt in his heart was felt through his body.

"Then, she needs to know. If she can access her powers and learn to harness them, she may be able to save herself," Caine explained.

"What is in it for you? She won't love a demon." Isaac's mind thought of Caine trying to seduce his niece and felt almost sick. Ava would be drawn to his energy.

"I don't want to fuck your niece. I will put it this way. I owe a friend a favor. This friend asked that I protect her from our world," Caine explained.

"Can you read my mind?" Isaac asked tentatively.

Caine nodded. Isaac knew demons normally wouldn't reveal their powers, but if he was going to pull this stunt off for Caine would have to break the rules.

"She needs protection. The cards have never been wrong and they have shown despair and death for her tonight," Isaac continued.

"She does, if there is a war brewing between the hunters and us, she is vital to the continuance of our race." Caine was business.

The two men continued to talk. How would they get Ava to even listen to this? She was rational most of the time, except when it came to her romance novels. She wanted to be swept off her feet by some alpha male character that would put his life on the line for her.

"She will not take easily to this."

"I don't care, she needs to understand. I will make her, if you won't." There was a quick heat in the room, as if a flash fire ran through everything. It was a warning, promise, and threat wrapped into one statement.

Uncle Isaac was the first to notice her. He stood straighter than usual and cleared his throat. The other male, Chris, the one who ran into her at the school was there. Why was he in Uncle's shop, and whom were they talking about?

Chris turned his head and nodded to Ava with a sly smile. She wondered if he could hear the sudden change in her heartbeat. He was a walking felony for looking the way he did.

"We'll continue this later," The Greek God of a man uttered another promise.

"I look forward to it." Isaac's voice was false, and from Ava's experience, more conversation with Chris was not what he wanted.

Chris turned and walked out of the shop without another word to either of them. Ava took the time to approach her uncle.

"Uncle, why was Chris in here?" She cocked her head to the side.

"Chris, right. We were just having a discussion, Ava dear. Shall I close up a tad early so we can go home? I think I want some citrus tea tonight." Isaac came from the counter and started flipping locks and entering security codes.

Once he was done, they set out. This evening, Isaac hailed a cab for them.

"Uncle, why was Chris there? It didn't look like you wanted him to be there," Ava noted. She was trying to curb her hunger for knowledge.

"My dear, you walked in on the tail end of a disagreement between Chris and me." His words were guarded.

"It sounded to me as if he was threatening you." She glowered at him in the dark cab,

"On the contrary, I am debating about hiring him to guard something quite precious. He is quite the security guard, apparently. How do you know him, dearest?"

"We literally ran into each other at school."

"I see." She could hear suspicion in her uncle's voice.

"What did you hire him to guard me?" It was her turn to play twenty-questions.

"You will see soon enough, dearest. A piece of my most cherished and prized possessions. It will be clear soon." He patted her hand to show the conversation was done, and he would not explain further.

After the cab arrived at their home and Isaac paid the driver, they went in to enjoy a full kettle of tea before bed.

Caine saw her once more. He heard her, and more importantly, heard her heart. She was an attractive little thing, but he would not reciprocate those fantasies or emotions. Isaac sounded disgusted that a demon might even think of being interested in his niece. Caine guessed it would be how any father felt about his daughter.

When Isaac and Ava left, Caine stayed close, shimmering in the shadows. The hunters would be out at night. Most deals were struck at night. There had to be a window where they could reach into the soul and claim it for their faction. The hold each demon faction on earth had been directly related to how many deals they had completed and would be cashing in on, so to speak. Hunters would break these deals by killing the demon responsible. As long as there had been demons making deals, there had been hunters. Lately, though, the hunters became offensive rather than defensive. Demons were being hunted and killed in the most painful ways the hunters could imagine.

Avaraz would hate him, surely, but the protection spells, the hiding spells, and anything else he had put in place would be broken soon. Ava could be hidden from other demons so she could live a normal life, but her own powers were manifesting. She would be powerful and quite useful for the demonic side. The hunters would see her as a threat and she would die slowly without understanding why until her last breath.

Once they were safely back inside, the demonic scent from Ava disappeared. He let the magic flow and shimmered back down to hell.

Avaraz could see Caine coming before Caine was amongst the demons in hell again. Avaraz could see the future. Which is why he was spared death and given an eternity shackled and tortured.

"My friend, is all well? Your heart is heavy." Avaraz noted.

"Yes, it is. The hunters seem to be running rampant above. There have been attacks, and half breeds are being slaughtered now, as well," Caine explained, his tone indicating he hoped Avaraz would appreciate this.

"You have seen my daughter." It wasn't an accusation, just a statement.

"Yes, she is coming into her powers. They are growing exponentially."

"She is in danger?" He already knew the answer was yes.

"Yes, the scent of power is strong on her. I fear if the demon hunters come within any distance of her, they will scent her and claim her, even though she is unaware of her nature." With those words from Caine, Avaraz sighed heavily and weighed his words carefully.

"Perhaps a short life is better than an imprisoned one," Avaraz replied.

"I am sorry my friend. I cannot let her die. We are going to need her for war against the hunters," Caine muttered his apology.

"You will bring my daughter into hell when you swore to me to protect her from this life?" The tone shifted from nearly defeated to scathing and protective.

"To save her and our kind, yes, I will defy you. We fought alongside each other for eons, but I disagree with you on this. You are thinking selfishly which is what got you strapped to this wall, never to be released."

"Then you condemn her to death." Avaraz turned his head away and would not utter another word to his onetime comrade.

"I wanted to bring her to see you. Perhaps, you could answer questions for her. But now, I may not bring her down here to see what a pitiful excuse for a demon you have become. Your selfish emotions would let the hunters claim our species, and most likely her, just for sharing your blood. Hunters are indiscriminate. Aware or not, they will kill all demons they meet." Caine departed.

Avaraz was now alone. He would go to his daughter once again this evening.

Ava and Isaac had spent hours conversing over tea. She brushed her teeth and changed into her pajamas. Then she climbed into bed and drifted off when another nightmare began.

There was kicking and screaming. A familiar hand cupped her mouth. It was her stranger...her father. His eyes bore down into hers.

"Ava, I need you to listen to me closely. We do not have much time. My power is dwindling greatly."

"What's wrong?" she begged.

"You are in grave danger," he spoke urgently.

"Tell me who. Tell me what!" she demanded.

"Trust in Caine. He will do what is right. Remember, evil is within. You cannot tell by a look," her father warned.

"What does that mean?"

"You are an astral projector. You can send yourself to other places, soul and all. You are also an empath, and a seer. You have many powers you have not uncovered yet, my child, all of my powers, as well as the saving grace of your mother."

"Who is the evil?" she asked again.

"Be prepared. You will have to fight for your life or face death on All Hallows' Eve," he continued as if he hadn't heard her.

"Father, please tell me. Who is the evil?"

"I fear the evil is already in your life. I cannot see them." He sounded pained.

"Please."

"My daughter, please know I love you. I tried to keep you safe. The hunters are coming." His words came faster.

"Father, please!" she shouted.

"I must go. When I have more strength, I will return to you. Isaac knows." He reached his hand out and cupped her cheek softly. *"Ava, you have grown up into such a beauty. It is truly a wonder to see you. You look so much like your mother."*

The spot where he touched began to burn her. She smelled what she thought was sulfur. The pain from the burn caused her to scream.

As usual, her screams woke her up. The pain remained on her face and in her heart. She desired to know her father so badly, but her mind was now playing tricks on her. The biggest thing on her mind was what he said. "Isaac knows" what did the dream mean by that? Dare she ask? Would Uncle Isaac think she went crazy if she did?

Ava got out of bed, the words still echoing in her brain. She went to the bathroom, shaking her head while she was walking, because she thought she was going crazy. Was she going to ask her uncle what her dream meant? She splashed water on her face to calm herself down, but when she went to pat her face dry she felt an excruciating pain radiate from where she pressed the towel. She dropped the towel into the sink and flipped on the light nearby. When she gazed back in the mirror, she gasped. She was burned, and burned bad.

There was more screaming. Her vivid nightmares were getting worse. There was no way to dismiss this as anything but a burn. Ava reached up to touch it. Her fingers were cool on the now throbbing part of her face. Her hands trembled as she went to her uncle's room. She planned on shaking him awake if she had to.

In Ava's mind, there was no way this conversation could wait until the morning hours. She had officially gone insane. She was afraid to go back to sleep.

CHAPTER 3

Ava's frantic voice brought Isaac out of his deep sleep cycle. He awoke with a start.

"Is everything all right, Ava?" He sat up fast.

"Uncle, what is wrong with me?" She burst into tears

Isaac rubbed his eyes. "What do you mean, my child? There is nothing wrong with you"

His long, deft fingers brushed through her hair in an attempt to comfort her, Ava's sobbing broke his heart. What could be the matter? Was it her nightmares? Were they getting worse? He waited for Ava to talk. Her body trembled with the terrible cries she held in.

"Ava, please tell me what is wrong."

"I'm different. I've known it all along. What is wrong with me? You know, Uncle. You know." Her tone was almost accusatory.

"What?"

"What is wrong with me? The visitor in my dreams is my father. He said you knew. You know what is wrong with me!"

"Ava calm down." He sat forward more.

"I will not calm down! I feel like I'm going insane!" Ava began pacing back and forth.

A heavy sigh escaped Isaac's chest. "Ava, we are not going to talk about this in my bedroom. Go downstairs and put on the kettle."

Her violet eyes pierced him. They were the shape of her mother's, just a different color. The beautiful purple orbs were locked on him. The evidence of her mother's lover was in there, the red demonically influenced. The young woman he had raised had no clue. He had lied to her for her entire life about her origins, but now it seemed he could not hide it any longer. She left his room. Before he rose from his bed, he said a quick prayer. How do you tell someone they are a half-demon? How could he tell her she was born of the things people feared most? That her mother was in love with a monster? How could he deliver this information to the girl he considered his daughter?

He stood, put on his robe, and went to the kitchen. Without a sound, he took in the sight of her. She was hunched over, both of her hands holding her head up, her body still shaking from sobbing. She was scared. Isaac took one more breath and completely entered the room.

"Ava, I am glad you are sitting." His voice was collected, but his insides were tumultuous.

"Please I see him every time I sleep. I've even been getting injuries." She lifted the veil of her thick dark hair.

He gasped. "Ava, what happened?"

"My dreams, they're vivid. I got hurt." She shrugged.

"This is not right. Who hurt you?" He was fierce in his need to protect his ward.

"My father, in my dream he touched my face. I felt it burn and then I smelled sulfur." She stared at her hands.

"What?"

"Yeah." Ava would not look up.

"Your father was taken from your mother many years ago. While she was pregnant with you... when the war first started to amp up."

"What?" Ava sputtered the word.

"I knew your father well; so did the rest of our family. He wanted to marry your mother. She met him in the eighties. None of us knew the truth about your father till it was too late. Your mom was in love with him, Ava. She was a hopeless romantic. She believed everyone had a soul mate. If you ask me, your father may not have had a soul."

"What did he do that was so evil?"

"He was a demon, Ava. He lied to us at first. He called himself something else; Ivan, if I remember right."

"You're fucking with me."

"Ava, do not use such coarse language. It is not appropriate for a young woman to use such crass words." Isaac always tried to instill a certain amount of propriety into her. She was a very modern young woman, much to his dismay.

"I'm sorry. You can't be serious, Uncle, a demon?" She looked up at him. His sincerity shone through his eyes.

"Yes, a demon. His name was Avaraz; perhaps why your mother chose Ava as your name. Your mother picked her name as your middle name, too. Maybe as a way to remind you of whom you would always be... Ava Christina, my Ava." Isaac ended with a fond thought. Ava was the closest thing he'd ever had to a daughter.

"Who is Caine?" she blurted.

"You've met Caine?" His eyes widened.

"In my dream, my father brought him up. He said to trust him." She got up to get the kettle from the heat.

"Right." He was obviously trying to figure out how to tell her and her calm unnerved him. "He is another demon."

"And in this demon world, Uncle, what does Caine have to do with me?" she questioned, her tone was near whimsical, like she thought it was all a joke, or a continuation of her dream.

"Caine has been sent by your father as protection. He was in my store recently to talk to me about it. Since you have become more intimate with your demon half, the measures I have taken to secure you are becoming futile. They will soon be able to sense you by your powers," Isaac explained.

"Powers? Like what? Do I puke green like that one movie?" she mused.

"No, your father was a seer. He was valuable to their council because he could see the futures of each person. He developed, and eventually, he could astral project to other planes. That is how, I suspect, he is contacting you in your dreams."

"Oh, really, so I could poof to Italy for pizza if I wanted?" She rolled her eyes.

"No, Ava, you are in no condition to talk about this," Isaac chastised. She woke *him,* and now she was being difficult.

"I can't sleep. I'm afraid, and your stories are making me feel better. Tell me more about my mom and dad. You can leave out the demon part. That's not really fairytale material." She prepared his tea from memory; dunking the bag a few times and leaving it in the cup for him.

"Ava, I wish this was a fairytale gone wrong, but it isn't. It is the truth. I have letters for you from your mother. I will retrieve them from the shop when it's daytime." He sipped his tea.

Ava remained silent while Isaac explained her life; where she came from and what her father was. He spun such a wonderful tale. She smiled into her cup and thought of what a wonderful book it would make. He mentioned that Caine had been to his store. She could imagine that shopping session. A huge man with horns and hooves walking into his store, scaring off his regular patrons, she had to laugh at that thought alone.

When they were both done discussing what Ava believed to be a placating story he constructed from his many nights of reading, she let herself believe in it for a moment only because he was so serious. After she cleared the table, she sat back down, a hot tingle at the bottom of her spine. What if he was serious? Something told her that he was. She felt another tingle down her spine.

She made her way back to her room, yet remained unable to sleep. She lay in her bed and stared at the white ceiling above her. Every bit of texture, she attempted to memorize. She was doing mindless things in order to quiet her racing thoughts. Ava's mind kept flitting back to her uncle's words. He spoke as if he were as sure of her future as he was of her past. Could she really be a demon? She was decent looking. She was not evil. Sure, she had a few days every month when she was an intolerable bitch, but what female didn't?

Eventually, her body calmed down and she went to sleep tossing and turning for the rest of the night. Words kept echoing in her mind. When the darkness reclaimed her, her dreams were just as vivid as before. But this time, it wasn't Avaraz that came to her – it was her mother.

She was sluggish when she woke the next morning. Her dream had been much of the same, a fiery torture which shook her to her soul. Avaraz was her father, her mother loved him, and she would have powers beyond her wildest imagination. All she needed, was a teacher. Ava ran her hands through her wild hair. She couldn't believe she was giving what her uncle had said in the wee hours of the morning any thought. Ava wrote the information down in her journal. If anyone ever read it, she would be locked in an asylum.

It did make sense, though...

After Ava's cell phone chimed with a text from Dom, she realized the time. She had spent most of her day lost in thoughts. She battered the thought to the back of her head and began to get ready for work. She needed to concentrate. The bar would be busy, as there was a popular live band playing tonight and she had a lot of prep work to do to ensure everything would run somewhat smoothly. She pulled her hair into two flirty braids. Wisps of hair escaped, gently framing her face. She dressed in her favorite jeans, boots, and t-shirt then headed out the door. Her uncle had already left for his store. His demeanor was somewhat defeated. She didn't want to make it worse.

Talking about her mother always made them both depressed.

Isaac was unable to go back to sleep after Ava's intrusion. He was now forced to tell her about her mother, and give Ava the letters his sister left for when she was truly ready. Isaac doubted if she would ever be truly ready to hear the truth. She was so strong, but so young at the same time. He opened the safe and pulled all the letters out, each numbered. He had read each one before, so he would know when the time was right. Caine was coming in to see him. Isaac may hate the bastard, but Ava needed to know how to protect herself. Caine was the only demon he knew who would be able to protect Ava from the hunters, now that she was coming into her own powers.

The letters smelled like his sister. He smiled as he thought of her writing them. She had known her end was coming. As always, she wanted her daughter to be prepared. Many things were set in place before Ava's birth. He promised to always take care of his niece. He started his electric kettle.

Caine stepped into the shop. He could smell the nerves coming from the aged man.

"You told her?" he questioned.

"Yes, I told her." Isaac's voice shook.

"What did she say?" Caine's brow rose.

"She laughed it off. I don't think she believes me. I am giving her these letters, tonight, when I go home."

"Then I shall go home with you. The magical shields are almost down. I can taste the power coming from your house. If I can pick it up that easily, you can be sure that a hunter could, as well," Caine warned.

"I understand, and yes you might want to. I will introduce you with your real name. She will have to understand and realize, perhaps, that you can show her what powers she possesses," Isaac suggested delicately. He did not want to piss off a demon, after all.

"I will teach her what I need to and nothing more. She will also be expected to submit to training." He was throwing out terms as if he owned the female.

"I doubt she will be happy with us making decisions for her, but we can try to sway her toward the decision softly, yes?" Isaac's voice cracked with worry.

"I can sway a woman to do nearly anything," Caine stated matter-of-factly.

"You will not persuade my niece to do anything she does not wish to do. Your kind seduced my sister and it led to her death. My niece will not share the same fate." Isaac was standing up to Caine to protect the child, interesting.

Sometimes, humans could surprise him. Caine chuckled low. "If I wanted your niece, I would have already had her. I have respect for her father and she, frankly, seems too demure for my tastes. I will come over tonight. You will prepare her." Caine was laying out his rules.

"Very well. Now please leave my store and let me do what I need to leave early." Isaac dismissed the rest of the conversation, which needed to take place.

Caine turned and walked out of the store, once more. After tonight, he would not need to conceal himself any longer, she would know the truth and she would have her ultimatum.

Ava was early for work. Instead of waiting for Dom to give her orders, she went straight to slicing and stocking everything they would need. The band would be drawing a crowd. Ava spaced out, still wondering about her dream. After a few hours of her mindless work, the band arrived for sound check. She let herself listen for a moment while they tested the equipment. After a few more hours, the band took a break. It was time for the public to be allowed in. Dom came out and nodded to the security team to start letting everyone in. Ava had another hour until she was off. She was getting tired, so she began to count the minutes.

Dom came up behind her and goosed her waist.

"Dammit, Dom!" she squealed.

"Hey, beautiful." He kissed her cheek.

"Hey, yourself." She nudged him.

"I want you to head out early, cut some hours, you know the drill." Dom's eyes flashed back and forth from the door to Ava. The hair on her neck stood up, but she did want to go home, so she didn't argue.

"Fine, I'll go. You got this handled, so I can count down the till and get out of your hair?" she asked.

"Oh, you know I got this, baby." His term of endearment made her smile.

Truth be told, Dom had starred in many of Ava's midnight fantasies. She imagined squirming under his touch again. The way his eyes would glow and his skin glistened was too beautiful not to think about.

She counted down her till and grabbed her stuff. On the way out, she caught the scent of Tonya's perfume coming from the manager's office. She must be figuring her till, too. The rank, designer knock-off perfume was more than Ava could take. She shuddered and turned, leaving the bar from the back entrance that led to the street from the alley.

Ava walked home quickly. She was heated after looking at Dom, and her uncle wasn't home. He was not due for a couple of hours. She locked the front door and went upstairs to her room. Her heat was causing her thoughts to be impure. If she didn't do something, she was sure to repeat her mistake of sleeping with the boss, once again. It was fun, amazing, mind-blowing sex, but Ava needed to move on, and so did Dom.

After she closed the door to her bedroom, she turned on the radio just in case. She decided to set her mood by lighting candles and plugging her iPod buds into her ear. Before she lay down, she reached under her bed and pulled out the clitoral vibrator she had spent a pretty penny for. Her uncle had almost intercepted the package. Ava shuddered at the memory of that horrible day. No, it was time to push that memory from her mind and enjoy one of her few moments alone.

Slowly she began to undress herself. Her fingers ran over her tender skin. It was warm to her touch and only got more intense. By the time she removed her bra and panties, her sex was pulsing to the music in her ears. Was that her imagination? Most likely, but was she going to stop to think about it? No. Ava's hands caressed the bare flesh of her breasts, she felt them stiffen under her fingertips, as if her core was jealous her hips pushed forward and begged for attention. The song was slow and sensual, one hand stayed on her breasts alternating between each one giving them both much-needed touches.

The many times Dom and Ava had been together crashed into her mind. When she thought of his smile looking up at her after he nipped at the tender flesh of her hip and moaned out softly, barely audible. She pinched the flesh of her hip between her index finger and thumb in an attempt to recreate the sensations he made her feel. She remembered how he bowed his head and seemed to praise the gods for her and her body as if her sex was a meal that he loved to devour. She whimpered out again as the scene morphed in front of her eyes.

The skin of the male darkened slightly, the shoulders broadened, and the muscles bulged. It was her personal Adonis, the stranger she had run into. His body shifted at her hip, and his eyes pierced into her soul, the world stopped. She could feel the heat of his hand, the feel of the scruff on his face as it scratched her thigh. The need drove her further. She didn't want to lose his looks from her memory. Every time their eyes connected the color of Chris' changed. He was a beautiful man. He kissed her thighs and right above her apex. She squirmed beneath him. He whispered in what she could only imagine to be Greek and his tongue swooped over her quivering sex only to excite her more. He seemed to know just what to do, of course it was her fantasy, but she didn't doubt his sexual prowess, he oozed potent sex. The kind a girl would never forget. Ava opened her eyes to make sure she was still alone, because with her vivid imagination it felt so real.

Her finger traveled closer, she was teasing her own body. Ava relished in the journey and the destination. Fingers started to get closer to where she felt the most need. Her thumb started to focus on her clit; the bundle of nerves made her a quivering puddle at first contact. She continued to rub just her clit, only that small pleasure allowed at the moment. Just before she could finish and experience the release she stopped and reached for her vibrator. Quickly she put the batteries in and placed the cool egg against her clit, another moan echoed in her room. Just the temperature difference was making her body beg for the release.

A distinct buzzing sound started to fill the room and Ava jerked. Her hips pumped erratically once more. Pleasure was building, she was getting cranked up and since her vibrator was taking care of her down below, her hands went back to her breasts. She twisted, pulled, and tweaked her nipples in just the way she needed. Her legs fell limply to the bed as her orgasm got closer and closer. She was so close to cumming by her own device. She still had Chris in her mind, she imagined his tongue swooping and swirling around her clit. Her climax hit her hard. Ava's toes curled and her back arched off the bed. She was locked into the position as her release controlled her. The intensity compelled her to cry out, she couldn't move to turn off the vibrator. She bucked wildly and moaned out, "Chris!"

After she regained control of herself, she cleaned her toy and took a quick shower. She was still panting hard when she washed her hair. She chuckled, who needs someone to love them when she loved herself she thought. Ava finished her shower and dressed in a pair of yoga pants and camisole. She re-braided her hair and went to start the kettle; she had ten minutes till her uncle was due home and she had to apologize for her idiotic intrusion the night before. She sat at the table to wait, her knees drawn up to her chest.

Isaac stared at his home. Ava was inside and she would be waiting for him. He glanced at his watch again. Caine was by his side. The demon was eager to go inside to meet Ava and tell her of her true life. What would become of his niece, the only family he had remaining?

"Are you ready?" Caine asked.

"As ready as I can be. I love her as my own child. I do not want her hurt," Isaac expressed his worry.

"This is the best way to prevent that." Caine countered.

"I hope you are right. She can be a stubborn child, just like her mother. My sister was headstrong and in love with a demon. She wouldn't give him up." Isaac hated the memory, but he had to admit the truth.

"He gave up his life for her, as well. He is now bound and tortured; forever to be held weakened by the chains of Hell. She is not the only one who lost. She, at least, is at peace," Caine growled low. He had to remind Isaac, but Isaac's behavior proved he didn't really care what Caine or Avaraz had lost, only that his sister was gone and he needed to protect Ava.

Isaac led the way up the few stairs to the house and let them in.

"Please, come in, Caine," Isaac invited him as an attempt to remember his manners.

Caine only nodded and stepped into their home. He surveyed his surroundings.

"Ava, are you home?" Isaac called out for his niece.

"Yes, Uncle, I'm in the kitchen. The kettle is on. Please, come to me. I wish to apologize to you." She sounded so formal. It was just how he raised her, as a proper young woman.

"Yes, my niece." He spoke and hung his coat at the same time, motioning for Caine to follow him.

Isaac took the last turn into the kitchen with Caine on his heels. The two men watched as Ava almost flipped out of her chair. She covered her chest and Caine watched her movements, much to Isaac's dislike. His dark rumble filled the air.

"Wh-what is he doing here?" She pointed at Caine

"I brought him to help explain," Isaac stated.

"Explain what?" She crossed her arms over her chest.

"He needs to help explain your heritage, other than being Armenian," Isaac finished.

"What do you mean?" She was visibly confused.

"You're a demon; a half-breed, but still powerful enough to be hunted and killed by our enemies. You need training in order to survive the next week, let alone the rest of your life." Caine spoke as if he was already tired of the dance.

"Bullshit," she fired back.

"Fine, watch me." Caine shimmered from the left of Isaac to his right, then behind Ava.

"FUCK!" she screamed.

"AVA!" Isaac yelled. He acted as if he had never heard such language from her mouth.

"Uncle, did you not see that?" She shook from head to toe. She was terrified of the dark stranger she had just fantasized about.

"Do you want me to talk about the thoughts you had of me, or should I just presume you know what I mean?" Caine's eyes glowed with a seductive promise.

"No!" she yelped out.

Isaac was left befuddled at the comments being shared. His niece obviously didn't want him to know, so he naturally needed to. At that moment, his interest shifted from her identity to her thoughts. "Ava, what is the meaning of the thoughts he is speaking of?"

"Nothing, Uncle, he is very rude to intrude on them, if he is serious." Ava glared at them both.

"Very well then, Caine. Please continue." Isaac flourished his hand, giving the floor to Caine once more.

CHAPTER 4

Caine enjoyed the look of curiosity as it turned to one of fear on the child's face. She was attractive, but she was not for him. He tasted the air around her. It shifted through many grids. She was quick to change from anger to frustration, arousal, more anger, shock, and back to anger again. Ava was as strange to him as she was beautiful.

"Ava, you will listen to me or it will be your life." He spoke with urgency.

"This is all some stupid ass dream. I'm going to wake up and be late for school." She covered her ears.

"Stop denying it," Caine grabbed her arm hard and shook her, "I have promised Avaraz that I would watch out for you. You will listen to me or die by a Hunter's hand."

"Ow!" Ava cried when he shook her. There was pain, then panic in her emotional grid that he could read instantly.

Caine released her arm immediately.

"You will deal with this, Ava. You have to," Isaac spoke up again, his old eyes wary and full of emotion.

"I'll try," she promised. Her dedication to the old man was paramount.

"Now, listen. Close your eyes, Ava," Caine waited for her to do so. "I want you to feel the heat, feel the anger inside you. Can you feel it?"

Ava shook her head. "No, I can't."

"Try harder," Caine demanded.

"I am!" she shot back.

"You must want to die. You are acting weak." He began to circle her.

"Stop it!" Ava opened her violet eyes and pegged him with a glare full of hatred.

"That's more like it." Caine lifted Ava's hand using his power. It was surrounded by an electrical energy that resembled lightning.

Her eyes popped open, as she looked at her hand amazed. Then, just as fast as it appeared, it disappeared.

"I am here to save your half-breed life. Now, if you listen to me, you may be able to make it through these raids and attacks. But if you whine, fuss, or bitch at me in any way, you will not learn and you will die. I am not here to coddle you. You have been kept in the dark about your history for far too long to your detriment."

Ava was in shock still. Her life had just changed dramatically. She saw the current run over her hand, she felt the anger boil, the rage ready to come out and attack Caine. She blinked down at her hand while he talked to her. "This is…"

"Strange?" Caine completed her sentence.

"To say the least."

"Get over it fast, princess, because you have a lot to learn."

At some point after his last outburst, Isaac had slipped from the room, leaving Ava alone with Caine. She became red faced at the thoughts of him between her legs on loop in her mind. He was sex in your veins and she could not resist looking him over once more.

"Quit gawking at me, child." She wondered why he used the word "child" so much with her.

"Okay… what do I do now?" she asked.

"You will ask me any questions you have about demons, or hunters, and I will answer to the best of my ability. Then, we will begin training. We have no time to lose on stupidity. You need to be well informed, so think hard, child." Again, his use of child was really starting to annoy her.

"First thing, can you please call me Ava? I hate being called child." Her tone was petulant, which must have amused him, because his luscious lips turned up in a smile.

"Fine then, Ava." His tongue caressed her name with sensuality.

"Th...Thank you," she stuttered, she tried to calm her thoughts. He was a demon. That's why he was having this effect on her. He was a demon and so was she.

"Calm your nerves. You need to start learning"

"You said something about a Hunter. What is a Hunter?" This seemed to be the most pressing danger.

"A Hunter is someone who hunts demons to kill the race. What many don't understand is we are a necessary evil. If everyone were an angel, who would be bad? Just like if it never rained, what would be a sunny day?"

The words made sense to her. Oddly, she felt as if she knew about it. "Is it like the whole life's duality; good and evil, light and dark?" she ventured.

"Yes, only the darkness isn't empty in this case." He rumbled a low chuckle.

"I see..." she trailed off.

"Do you want me to answer questions as they come or have a designated time so you do not disturb your training?" Caine walked closer, towering over her.

"I'll ask when they come. I'm still processing." Ava wrapped her arms around herself while she looked up at Caine.

"Good, then let us begin. You must harness your anger, young... Ava," he caught himself.

"Why are my eyes purple?" she blurted.

"You must have had blue eyes from your mother. The demonic gene mingled with it. Demon eyes are red normally."

72

She was silent after that.

"Is that all you have to question me about for now?" he asked.

"For now," she echoed his last words.

"Good, then focus on the anger."

Ava tried to collect herself. She stood in the small room and closed her eyes. She could feel her body connect to the anger deep within. Her stomach coiled at the purity of the rage she was just now feeling inside of her.

"Good, good, anger is the quickest way to trigger your demonic half. Keep concentrating." She was starting to let up and he caught her.

"Now, visualize the power. What do you see? Do you see the electricity, the bolts of energy?" he continued.

She could sense the energy twisting around her hand, engulfing it. The moment she stopped concentrating, the electricity snapped and fell away. She cursed in dismay.

"You need to concentrate!" Caine's voice boomed.

"I'm trying!" Ava fired right back. She was positively pissed.

"No, you are not! You are acting weak! Your father would be ashamed his daughter couldn't even create an energy ball," he growled.

Ava charged at him with those words. "Oh, yeah, and let's talk about what a fantastic father he's been to me," her words dripped with disdain.

The girl surprised him. His thought of her being fiery came back. "No, he hasn't been a good father to you, but my friend is chained to one of the hell barriers so you could be safe."

"What?" She looked abashed at his words.

"You heard me. Your father is chained to a wall to keep you safe. The elders wanted to bring you in and make you one of us, or kill you, whichever proved to be more fun. But, no, he doesn't love you at all, you selfish little girl."

She stood in silence.

He strode around her, taking in every curve of her, the apple shape of her ass, and the perfect upside-down heart. Caine's eyes went to her hair, long luscious mahogany locks that cascaded around her. Her violet eyes drew him in closer. Before he knew it, they were chest to chest. A growl rumbled in his chest.

"What are you doing?" she asked, her voice was husky with desire.

"What you want me to do?" he replied with a devilish smirk.

"What do you think that is?" Her eyes still glared at him.

"This." The word was so simple. He gave into the tension quickly building between them.

Caine's powerful arm wrapped around her waist and tugged her against his muscular chest. Her full lips were soft against his. When she didn't push him away that was his cue to continue. Caine's lips ravaged Ava's.

His massive fingers fanned along her delicate back as he pulled her tighter to him.

To his surprise, she was just as passionate. Caine almost forgot she was a half-breed demon. She was the same temperature as a human, and just as soft, too. She was not a soul to make a conquest of. This was the daughter of a demon, one that they desperately needed. His lips synched with hers. He bunched her shirt in his hand, tempted to rip it off. His free hand cupped her exquisite backside and lifted her against him. It was like she could read his mind. Her legs wrapped around him for stability and she pressed closer as if she ached for him. This little girl was surprising him. In lithe movements, he walked like the predator he was to the closest wall and leaned her against it. The scent of lust was coming from her like a full-blown demon. Caine could see what would happen. He could bed her if he just spoke the words of a lover, he had said them so many times as a lie it would be simple to say them one more time. Then, Avaraz's request came to his mind. He was to protect her – not bed her.

Her tongue was still coaxing his in her mouth. She was rolling it with definite natural skill. Caine's mind became clear. Ava's body was pressed against his. The intensity of the forbidden attraction bit into him. He lowered her to the ground and pulled away. Her eyes pegged his. The anger was gone. The need for sex resided.

"Why did you stop?" The sound of wounded pride seeped into her voice.

"Because this isn't helping your training. I proved I could have you. Your emotions can be swayed. You can be easily distracted." He wished he could spare her the hurt in her eyes. "You bastard." She screamed.

Her fist curled and launched forward. Caine made no motion to stop it. She had every right to be angry with him. He was a cad for what he had done, and even more so for what he said.

"I am a demon. I am not innocent, Ava. You need to train. You need to quell your desires." Caine's voice was regretful.

"If you don't want me, what's with that?" She pointed at his erection straining to be freed from the cage it was confined to.

"That is of no consequence to you. That is simply a physical reaction," Caine dismissed her.

"Bullshit." Her glare returned.

"It is time to train, not doubt my ability as a demon of lust." He squared off with her. He glared in return.

"I really hate you, right now," her pride spoke.

"Good. You need to have anger." The thought of being hated didn't faze Caine.

"Why?" she asked.

"That is how a demon is. We are powerful when angry. It is like the angels are at peace when they are happy and calm. They just are."

"Why is that?" Again she asked a question.

"Why don't you just keep asking me questions? Demons are filled with ire. We thrive in hell. We embrace the anger, and live better." He sounded clear-headed.

She stopped talking for just a moment. Her bright eyes closed, and when they opened, he could see the pain in them.

"What is wrong, Ava?" he asked, ready to kick himself for having to hurt her.

"My father… he's in hell to protect me." When she spoke, he was unsure if it was a question or a comment. Something had gotten to her.

"Aye, he is. He is powerful and was able to cloak his mind enough, so that you were never found out. He became a prisoner to the wall. A disgraced demon. He fell in love with a mortal and wanted to stop making deals. A demon lives to make the deal."

"Oh." Her word was small and loaded with so much emotion.

"Your father loves you. He told me he visits you often. Even the wall cannot keep him away from you." Caine tacked on.

"He's coming to me in my dreams?"

"Yes, he loves you and wanted to warn you of the war. He has the power of prophecy. He predicted plenty of events in the war which have already come to pass, and he wants to prevent your death." He started to give details.

"I'm going to die?" The small voice made Caine look twice. It had not come from the woman who had just kissed him as fiercely as she just had, had it?

"If you are left unprepared. The battle is mounting, Ava. This is serious. You can live. You can thrive as a demon. You just need to train." He had softened his voice.

"What kind of powers will I have?" she ventured.

"Most likely your powers will mirror those of your father, perhaps telepathy, premonition, the energy balls, and everything in the lust demon repertoire."

"Anything cool?" she asked.

"You don't think those are cool? Mortals, you believe everything is like the television shows." He chuckled.

"Can I freeze things? Do that shimmery thing you did?"

"You will be able to shimmer soon, with practice. Freeze things? I assume you might be able to if you were born with that power. You will be able to use telekinesis, for certain."

"That's the ability to move things with your mind, right?" She cocked her head to the side in the most endearing way.

"Yes, television has that right." He rumbled and laughed afterwards.

"I want to work on that!"

"Any particular reason?" he asked.

"Just a bitch at work I would love to use it on." She gave her own smirk. Her lips turned up and Caine's followed.

78

"You are not allowed to use any powers on mortals until you have learned control. You do not want to harm an innocent, do you?" His left brow rose.

"No, I don't really want to harm anyone," she confessed.

"You will not have to. We contract souls. We must first have a window, such as a Wall Street broker who wants power. He is greedy in his heart, coveting things that he does not need. A demon could make a deal for his soul to give him the power he needs," Caine explained, "and when it comes time to collect, you call the soul, and it comes. No pain."

"I have one more. I am basically being tapped to join you, correct?"

"Yes, you are being tapped to join your people."

"Why?" The silence hung between them, her desperation to know clearly written on her face.

"The hunters I told you about. We need to protect ourselves better."

"Then we should begin training. Just so you know that I can't really fight." She bit her lip and looked down as if she were ashamed of her innocence.

Cute, Caine thought.

"Time to get angry again." Caine was almost gleeful; his soldier's instinct was coming forth.

After hours of Caine attempting to connect Ava to her powers on a deeper level, she fell onto the sofa exhausted. He had tried to keep her angry, and the amount of hatred and anger she had to concentrate on was emotionally and physically draining. She had learned a small thing in comparison to what she had left. The electricity ball was forming in her hand and she could run the power over her skin.

She picked up her water bottle before she looked at the clock.

"It's almost five in the morning," she noted.

"That it is. Later today, after you have rested for a couple of hours and attended your daily schedule, you will come to me again." His dictator tone was back.

"Are you kidding? I am exhausted. You should let me sleep today." She whined.

"We have no time to lose, Ava. You are to come to training today." Caine was firm.

"Where should I go? We can't keep practicing here. It isn't safe for Uncle."

"I have secured a dilapidated gym. I will prepare it to host us for your training. You will be able to access your powers without having to worry about hurting anyone." Caine took the towel from Ava's hands and wiped his own face.

"Thanks," she said sarcastically.

"You're welcome," he tossed it back.

Caine stood to leave. He grabbed his coat and shrugged it on. "Ava, you will come to me or I will come find you."

"Promise?" she shot back out of reflex.

"Yes." With that being his last word, he turned. Leaving Ava alone, he shimmered out.

"Damn demon, showing off." she grumbled and walked up the stairs to shower.

When Ava was done with her ablutions, she hit her pillow and had the sweetest love affair she could remember.

Ava could have slept for an eternity and it wouldn't have been long enough. She had another nightmare. Michael was burning in a sea of fire again. Her dream had felt even more real. The fire had licked her hand this time. She clenched her hand and dismissed it as her powers not being under control.

Her uncle called for her from the kitchen when he heard her footfalls.

"Yes Uncle?" She asked when she rounded the corner to the kitchen.

"I need to talk to you about your mother." He said gravely.

She sat down noiselessly. Ava wanted to know everything about her mother, but her uncle had rarely talked about his departed sister.

"Your mother was lively," he began.

"Yes, Uncle, I know she was always happy. I want to hear a new story. Did she know of my father's life?" She didn't want to say demonic lies.

"Ava, she knew. You are named for both of them, Avaraz and Christina. Once you were born, your mother understood she was marked for death."

She sat in silence, soaking in the information.

"Christina loved Avaraz, even though he lied. He was sent to corrupt her. She still loved him. Perhaps, an earth bound angel could have saved a demon. Avaraz suddenly disappeared and Christina started seeing things in her dreams. She couldn't explain it, but she started preparing for her death. Only I knew of this. I prayed for her soul." Isaac rubbed his aged hand over his face.

"What happened?" She was thirsty for any knowledge of her mother.

"Your mother prepared for her death by writing her will; the one that led to me having and protecting you. She left me information and clues on how to protect you the best, and letters for your birthdays, and other special events in your life. Ava, she gave me the information on witches, demons, and old magic. That is how I have protected you. Hunters have been around New York for a long time. The spells I was given have cloaked you, so long as you have been innocent and without exposure to demons. I fear the cloaking spell will soon fail." He finished as a whisper.

"What?" Her pupils dilated in fear.

"The spells that have kept you off the demonic radar and the Hunters' radar will soon be failing because of Caine being near you. Others will be able to find you, and possibly take you, as they took your mother." Isaac sounded as if he regretted letting Caine come to Ava.

"Who killed mom?" she begged for the answer.

"I am positive it was the Hunters. They killed her because she smelled like a demon. Your father's scent was all over Christina and she was loyal. She wouldn't give up information about him, your existence, or demons in general. They would have tortured her for the information, and then killed her to bring the demon. Your father would have felt each and every evil thing they did to her. He was bonded to her in a cosmic way. Nothing could break that except for death, when he finally opened his wings to welcome her." Isaac gulped and looked at his niece.

"They killed her?" Ava's voice trembled with tears that were unbidden.

"Yes."

"Then, I will exterminate every one of those fuckers I can," she vowed.

"You cannot hunt them, Ava. You must protect yourself and live, because that is what she wanted for you." He warned.

"No, she wanted me to live as I choose. She wanted me to live and know the truth, Uncle." Ava fussed with her hair.

"Ava…" he began.

"No, Uncle, they stole her from me. I am going to get my revenge. I need to go train." She stood back up and left the room.

Isaac had nothing to do but pray for his beloved niece the way he had prayed for his sister.

"Please, don't let her have died in vain. Please, watch over my niece." He had to wonder if his words would even be heard now.

Ava went to demon training, as she deemed it. After another intensive session, she was able to throw energy balls, deflect them, and even began to shimmer. The air around her would become displaced as she began to disappear. With a little more practice, she would be able to vanish completely.

Caine had pushed her harder than she ever felt before. She pushed right back. He reminded her, every chance he got, that her life was on the line. She was not allowed to fail.

She was just getting out of the cab, when she heard his voice.

"Ava!" He waved her over.

"Michael!" She was surprised.

"Hey, you weren't in school today." He halted a few feet away.

"Sorry, I overslept, so I decided just to hit the gym," she offered a reason for her disheveled appearance.

"Are you okay?" he asked.

"Yeah, I'm fine."

Michael stepped forward and put his hand on her skin. His thumb stroked her forearm. "Ava, you bailed on our project today." His tone was accusatory.

"I'm sorry. I told you I overslept." She shifted and tried to pull her arm back.

"You're my partner. I need to be able to depend on you." His grip tightened.

"You're hurting my arm, Michael." She warned.

"You fucking skipped out on me and expect me not to be mad?" His nostrils flared.

"I didn't mean to!" she yelled her words.

"Did you really go to the gym or were you just too busy to notice you had responsibilities?" His snide comment hit Ava like a ton of bricks.

"Excuse me?" She could feel the anger rising in her throat, but Caine's words calmed her.

"You heard me." Michael glared.

Ava ripped her arm out of Michael's firm grasp. She could almost feel her skin bruising. He'd had her arm in a vice grip. She shook with fury. She was tempted to use her newfound powers against him.

"Get the hell away from me," she shot at him.

"Go back and fuck whoever you skipped the project for." He seemed to have changed in just a few moments. *Perhaps, Michael is bipolar,* she thought, then again she wasn't a mental health professional, she only knew what she saw on television and that was always a bad idea to judge something by the media surrounding it.

Without a conscious decision, Ava moved as fast as she could and backhanded Michael. She was beyond irritated, exhausted, and his insults were cruel.

"I will forget you came here tonight. But you are to never, and I mean NEVER, talk to me like that again or you will regret it." There was an edge to her voice she had never used before.

The demon was rubbing off on her.

Michael turned to leave in a huff. Ava stood her ground, watching him get into his car and peel off into the night. When he was out of view, she rolled up the sleeve of her sweatshirt and looked at where he had grabbed her. There were ugly purple bruises already forming, each one a spot where his fingers had dug into her. Ava flexed her hand and forced herself not to cry over the intense physical and mental pain.

"What a fucking jackass." She licked her teeth and went inside to find her uncle to warn him of Michael's new obsession with her whereabouts.

CHAPTER 5

Weird was the only way Ava could describe her run in with Michael. He was acting as if he were obsessed with her. He had flipped from being the sweet man she knew him to be, to this crazed lunatic she had witnessed just now. Could he have been drunk? But she would have smelled the alcohol on his breath, wouldn't she? She did work at a bar, after all. Perhaps he was high, or mixing his medications with drugs.

"Ava, what has preoccupied your mind tonight? Has Caine attempted to push his agenda on you?" Isaac came to her side and rubbed Ava's shoulders.

"No, Uncle, my friend, Michael, just scared me." She didn't want to alarm him.

"What happened?" he pushed.

"Nothing important, Uncle," she said, her tone was clipped, she was arguing internally whether or not to tell him, she had changed her mind now that he was in front of her.

"Very well, then. How about I make us some tea?" Isaac recovered swiftly and Ava experienced a pang of guilt.

She didn't want to worry her uncle. Ava decided she was not going to tell him what happened with Michael. She was sure tonight was a onetime event. She would go to school, and he would be waiting to apologize with either coffee or chocolate. Her body slumped into a nearby chair. She kept her arm under the table and rolled the sleeve of her sweatshirt back down so Isaac's prying eyes wouldn't see what Michael had done. What was she going to say? She decided on not telling him anything. Not bringing the subject up was for the best because she didn't want to upset him anymore than he already was.

Isaac was busy making the tea while Ava was lost in her thoughts. Perhaps she would ask Caine the next day about training more.

"Ava, you are distracted, but I shall leave it be. How is your training going?" he asked.

"I think it is going well. Do you think I should ask to train more so I can protect us both?" She was curious as to what her uncle would say on the matter.

"You spending more time with Caine is not something I like. Demons are the reason your mom was taken from us. I do, however, think you need all the skills you can attain as fast as you can get them. Please, see him more if it will help you learn to protect yourself better." Her safety was always of paramount importance to him.

"All right, Uncle," she said affectionately.

"Since you are spending so much time away, I have had to acquire new business leads to fill my time. I have one that will be taking me on a trip for the next week. I will be leaving tomorrow evening." Isaac filled both teacups on the table.

"Where are you going?" she asked as she took a sip.

"I have to attend a meeting in Rochester first, then I will be going along the coast. I will be collecting things and dropping off a few of my own along the way. We also have family sending in items to Miami for me to pick up." He swirled the liquid in his cup and looked into it.

"Why Miami?" she asked, "Isn't New York closer?"

"Yes, our port is closer, but Miami is warm and an old man needs time to stare at scantily clad women on a beach without seeming perverted, my young Ava." Isaac smiled.

"Just don't come home with a wife, okay?"

"If I find Miss June, I may, but I have no intentions of marrying," he continued.

"Eww!" She wrinkled her nose in mock disgust.

"You know you are the only woman I can put up with for more than a day, Ava. I could never replace you." He reached his hand across the table to comfort her.

"Thank you, Uncle. How long will you be in Miami looking at assets down there?" she emphasized the word *ass* in assets.

"I am thinking just a few days. I do have a store to run. I can't leave it closed for long. Business must be done." He nodded succinctly.

"Will you be here for breakfast tomorrow?" she asked.

"Yes, I will make you the normal breakfast for this situation; cinnamon rolls, bacon, eggs, and fresh orange juice, the classic comfort breakfast." He stood.

"Are you going to bed?" She cocked her head to the side to see the clock. It was just past eleven at night.

"Yes, not all of us are young with stamina like yours, child." He smiled at her.

"You are as young as you want to be, Uncle," she countered.

"Life has other plans." He kissed her forehead. "I will see you in the morning." He departed the kitchen and walked up the stairs.

Ava waited until she heard the door close before she pushed her sleeves up and went to wash the teakettle out. Her hand was under the flow of water from the faucet, waiting for the water to warm up. She hummed and thought more about Caine.

The thoughts started as uninvited memories of his bossy nature. It was intoxicating, how he loomed over her, his warmth always on her as he tried to access her anger. Then, the thoughts changed. She was living in her memory for a moment, lingering on the kiss they shared. It was passionate. She thought about how his arms had wrapped around her hips when his head ducked down to kiss her, and then her breath hitched as she thought about what his zipper had been hiding. She needed to calm down, but her thoughts refused to leave.

Holy cow, he must have been huge. If she had any doubt before, that kiss sealed the deal. He was massive inside everywhere. His muscles rippled through the shirt and his hard body was tight against hers for that brief moment. She had felt every bulge and every inch of his chest and abs. He was a mouth-watering specimen. Ava began to wonder how many women he bedded. He had a body which begged for women to be sinners. Who could resist?

"Shit!" She jumped and pulled her hand back hard as the water burned her skin.

Ava blushed. She felt sheepish over her silly mistake. She needed to stop letting herself daydream about him. He was off limits. That cocky attitude and wide smile was all she needed to secure her spot in hell… Caine was more trouble.

"You called?" a voice whispered in her ear.

Again, she jumped. "Dammit!"

He chuckled darkly. Even his laugh was sensual "You are jumpy today. Why is that?" Caine asked.

"Nothing, just that you're a sneaky bastard," Ava chastised him.

"You called me." Caine pressed himself into her back.

Warmth gushed and she wanted to press back into him. "I did?"

"What is this?" He reached out his hand and grabbed her arm. He lifted it into the light.

"It's nothing." She shrugged from his grasp. She noticed she was saying that a lot.

"You are bruised from someone's fingers." Caine's anger was growing.

"Yes, I am. It's none of your business." Ava shot back.

"You are my business now, Ava. I need to protect you, and I have failed." He was growing distant again.

"Someone grabbed me. He was drunk. I took care of it," she tried to end that conversation.

Caine was angry. He tried to quell his growl, but failed. Ava's head jerked back up and she looked at him. When he realized he failed to protect her from even a mortal's grasp it was a slap in his face. He began to internalize his fury.

"I didn't call you," Ava argued again.

"What?" He had forgotten already.

"I said I didn't call you. My cell phone is over there. Why are you here?" she asked again.

"Your body called me," he answered with a shrug.

"You can feel me?" she inquired

He nodded, still scowling.

"How?" she asked.

"Your body, it called to me. You are a very powerful half-breed. I felt the call while I was in hell." He was amused.

"I still don't understand."

"Ava, your body was calling to me. You wanted me here. You were summoning me subconsciously." His lips turned up in a smirk.

"I did?"

"Yes, you did. Now, what could you have wanted me for?" He flexed his pectoral muscles.

"I don't know." She shrugged and went back to the dishes to disguise her feelings.

"Yes, you do, silly girl." He pressed up behind her once more and felt the curve of her backside pressed against the front of his jeans.

He almost groaned.

Almost.

Ava was powerfully attracted to him. She couldn't deny it. He was beautiful, sarcastic, intelligent, and different. Her body called to him, so he said. Now, he was in her kitchen. They were virtually alone together, *again*. Caine wasn't pushing her to work harder. He was almost playful with her. The playfulness soon turned into something more teasing, more sensual. He was pressed against her, lust rolling off of him in thick waves. She shuddered softly at all the fantasies running through her mind. She dropped the teakettle into the sink and turned to face Caine. His smirk was very rewarding. She pressed herself against him.

"Ava…" he spoke softly, like a lover would.

"Yes," was her more than willing reply.

"Go get some sleep." He chuckled and backed up.

"What?" Her voice fell flat.

"You heard me. Go to bed. We have a busy day tomorrow. You will be going under live-fire." He beamed from ear to ear, then the air moved and he shimmered away, leaving her alone with her thoughts again.

Ava could feel the anger and frustration building inside of her. Why the hell did he get off on torturing her sexually?

Oh, that's right. He's a demon of lust.

A vase crashed against a wall, and a deafening roar sounded, "What do you mean she has been found?"

"Sir, the half-breed was found by a faction." A smaller voice trembled.

"Then, you will do your job. Find her, kill her, and make it look like a regular human did it." The first voice growled again.

"Yes, sir," the voice fell silent.

"Good, now you are dismissed. Get the hell out of my sight." The dominating voice spoke again.

There was no rebuttal from the weaker of the two. The air only shimmered as he disappeared.

"This little half-breed could be my undoing. He'd better take care of the problem, *before* it gets worse," the voice mused to no one else.

Demon training starts too early, the words were becoming her mantra. She woke up with her usual lethargic movements and slapped her alarm clock in anger until it stopped it's chiming. She dressed and went to meet Caine at the training facility, which was now her own personal hell. He was so strict, and the hot and cold action from the night before in her kitchen did not sit well with her. She was still thinking about it. Caine starred in her dreams again last night.

It featured him, an argument about her training, and her finally taking a stand against him. He was shocked when she started the contest. His arms were hesitantly around her, then suddenly it flipped and he was between her legs, pumping. owning, and taking what he wanted. She woke up panting loudly.

Ava entered the training complex and found Caine doing pull-ups on a bar. She stood in the background for a few moments, watching his body rise and fall as his arms worked. He was quite impressive, and with a sheen of sweat blossoming over each rock hard muscle, she was salivating. Her gulp was audible.

"Are you going to come in and train, or are you going to stay over there and count how many pull ups I can do?" Caine's deep voice boomed.

"I'm still trying to decide what I want to do," she shot back.

"I decided you would come in and take off your coat. I have a plan for you." He dropped down and his feet landed with a thud.

"After that?" She took off her coat and let it slide to the floor.

"You will be facing me in hand to hand combat." He walked up to her.

"You're shitting me?" she scoffed.

"No, I am not shitting you, Ava. Fight me," he pushed.

"Why?"

"If I am ever not around and a human attacks you, you need to know how to defend yourself. Even a demon uses hand to hand combat."

"Shouldn't I be concentrating on something more useful, like learning my powers?"

"No, just listen, you silly girl," he growled ever so slightly.

"Fine!"

"Assume your position," Caine ordered.

They began to play war games. She was horrible. Ava could barely make a fist. He laughed at her pitiful attempts to hit him. He worked with her for hours upon hours. She hit the mats hard. The only way she would learn to defend herself, is if she learned her lesson with blood; the only way she could. Caine laughed a few times at how she bounced when the ground met her ass.

"At this rate, you will tire out any human attacker." He chuckled.

"Really?" She attacked again. This time, she landed one fist to his jaw.

"Good." Caine's tone was one that made her believe he was impressed.

"Can I go home now?" she asked as the sweat fell from all of her pores.

"Yes, you may. You have made tremendous progress today. I have business I must tend to below, anyways. I was just about to suggest we end."

"Perfect, because I need a shower, then a bath, then a muscle relaxer or two," she elaborated.

"Go. I will contact you tomorrow morning. If you need me, call for me again." He nodded.

Ava watched the air change as the magic built and Caine shimmered away. She grabbed her clothes and started to walk away from the training gym. It was an abandoned factory on the outskirts of the city. She hailed a cab once she was far enough away and closer to civilization.

The cab dropped her off at her home, and she went inside to find her uncle. She forgot that he had left early in for his business meetings and mini-vacation.

Ava sighed and flipped the lock into place. Isaac would have a fit if Ava did not do so, even if she was able to send energy balls after anyone who entered.

She put a small crock-pot meal into her slow cooker and went upstairs. She decided because she would be alone for the night, she would take her shower then indulge in a bath with scented candles and salts. Ava started to run the water and undress slowly. There were light bruises forming. She hoped they wouldn't be visible the next day.

After she washed herself thoroughly, she rinsed out her shower to make sure it was clean, and then she plugged the drain. She stepped out to wrap her long hair in a towel, light her raspberry mint candles, and add the salts to dissolve. She turned on music as her last step in preparing her bath.

Ava slipped into the bath slowly once it was full. She hissed through her teeth at the heat. The water engulfed her body and the steam surrounded her. Her head gradually sunk down as she relaxed more and more. She inhaled deeply and let the hot water work wonders on her sore body while the music played softly in the background.

After she spent an hour soaking, she got out of the water. She had already warmed it up twice with fresh bursts from the faucet. Ava wanted to get some rest tonight. She still had to blow-dry her hair, handle the rest of her business, and check in with her uncle. She couldn't forget to call him.

She wrapped her body in a towel then took her hair out and started to brush it, her feet moving slightly. Ava was dancing to the song playing in the background. Once her hair was dry enough to sleep, she went to her room. The cold woods under her feet made her move double-time.

The lock was easy enough to break open. It barely took a flick of his wrist. A mask covered his face. He pulled it into place before he took his first step inside. There was music coming from what he imagined to be the upstairs bedroom. Silently, he walked up the stairs, sticking close to the wall to conceal his presence as much as he could. When the bathroom door opened, he crouched down into a striking position, but she went the opposite way.

He waited until she was in her room to move closer. He listened to every footfall, every heartbeat, and every movement he could track. The girl was humming. She didn't know her fate rested with him. The assailant felt bad. He was a criminal, and he was going to steal her from the world. He ducked into the bathroom, like the cad he was. He waited for her next move.

Her brown hair swung as she walked by his hiding spot. She reached in without looking to flip the light off. He edged forward ready to pounce on her if she returned for some reason. Tension corkscrewed through his muscles. He was ready. The knife in his hand would surely be enough of a weapon. He pondered mortality for a moment, but this score was too important to blow. If he didn't succeed, he would be killed and someone else sent to take her life.

In a swift movement, he crept into the hallway again. He avoided touching anything that could make noise and expose his whereabouts. She was on her way to the kitchen. He felt oddly exposed as he followed. He breathed shallowly to prevent excess noise. She put on a kettle of water and her hand lingered by the stove. This was the best chance he would have. He couldn't see any objects she could fight back with. The man stepped from the hall and quickly closed the distance from behind. His arm went around her neck and pulled tight. This started the rodeo.

Ava didn't hear anything or anyone behind her. Her mind raced with the events of late. She was still considering going on the run, but that would leave her uncle to deal with the consequences, yet again. A strong forearm squeezed against her neck and pressed hard. She immediately began to claw at it. Her oxygen was fading fast because of her panic. The person brought his other arm up and held her neck tighter. Ava panicked. She reached behind her in hope to gouge something important. She thought of a movie she had watched on cable recently. Her height helped her. She jammed the heel of her foot down onto the man's foot, elbowed his stomach as hard as she could, and then brought it up and into his nose. She brought her fist back and went for his genitals last. There was a gurgled howl of pain and she took his moment of weakness and grabbed her hot kettle and bashed it into the side of his head. The assailant dropped to the floor. She debated for only a moment then took off running. He grabbed her foot and she went sprawling onto the floor. She landed a kick to his face and scurried away from him. She ran into her room for safety.

She slammed the door, threw the lock into place, and willed her body to call Caine with all her might. She was calling him as hard as she could. At least, she thought she was. He wasn't responding fast enough. There was a loud thump against the door, and then another. The man must have been throwing himself against the door to break it open. She was scared. She could feel the fear in her throat.

"GET OUT!" she screamed.

"NO!" was the one word answer that was gruffly screamed back at Ava.

There was more noise. Ava knew she would have to either depend on Caine or handle this herself. She prepared for the worst. The door shattered into a few pieces and a body clad in black clothing and mask crashed through. There was an audible groan when he hit the ground. Ava surveyed her room fast. There was nothing she could strike him with again. She was going to have to expose herself, and her power, to a stranger.

She didn't know how it would go, but she had no other choice.

The would-be thief brandished a knife. "I could make this painless for you," he threatened.

"I could say the same." She backed up, attempting to buy time, as she tried to center herself.

No more words would be exchanged. Ava's breathing changed subtly as she keyed into her anger. The anger most powerful was the fact this person assumed she was weak. She licked her lips as he stalked forward. His eyes widened, like a deer caught in the headlights of a semi-truck. He lunged with the knife. She reacted quickly and attempted to strike him to force him to drop the knife. She failed at it and he had his arm wrapped around her neck once more, the knife against her artery.

She gulped when the fear bit off her words. The blade slightly cut into her neck. The copper smell of blood hit the air and she inhaled.

"This could have been easier." The voice was a gruff, unrecognizable whisper.

"It could have," she spoke through gritted teeth and finally she felt the energy start to build.

Ava closed her eyes and let the hatred flow through her entire body. The energy ball appeared in her hand. When she opened her eyes, it grew in size. She closed her eyes once more and visualized the energy running over her entire body. Before she could stop the thought, or control the level of electricity, she felt the knife tighten then fall away from her throat. A roar of pain came from behind her. It was so loud it hurt her ears.

Using all of her strength Ava got her arm up and clawed until she was able to push the arm away from her neck and using a calculated move Caine taught her she was able to knock the knife out of the assailant's hands. She wheeled back and kicked him. He was panting in pain. Ava reached down to grab the mask and reveal his identity. She could almost taste his panic, and it shocked her how much she liked it.

He pushed her back and scrambled up. The coward took off running. The anger had boiled over and she didn't know how to stop immediately. She launched an energy ball at his head. The fear caused him to run faster. He jammed his shoulder on the wall, which caused him to spin out the door and go spiraling down the stairs.

Ava ran to the front door she looked up and down the street for him, he was gone. She figured he just ducked down one of the side streets and was hiding and hyperventilating, it wasn't every day that someone threw a demonic ball of energy at your head.

Just as Ava went to investigate, Caine appeared with a scowl on his face.

"Did you call me, just so I could see you in your pajamas?" he growled.

"No, I called you because someone just held a damn knife to my throat," she fired back and lifted her chin to show the cut.

"WHAT?" Caine snarled.

"Yeah, someone broke into my house. I think they wanted to rob me, or just kill me," she tacked on.

"Give me your hand, show me." He stuck his large palm out.

"Uh, what do you want me to do?" Her adrenaline started to fall.

"You take my hand and go over your memory of the event. You just have to be willing to show it." He was exasperated. He needed to know what happened.

She took his hand and the memories began to flow into his mind. He was watching from Ava's point of view. She was in the kitchen thinking about Caine. Much to his surprise, it was pleasant thoughts about their kiss.

When the memory wrapped up, he was surprised Ava had control over a power ball the size she conjured, and the launch was priceless. He almost howled with laughter when she threw it at the man.

"You have one hell of an arm on you with that energy ball, Ava." He chuckled darkly.

"I almost get my neck sliced open and you laugh about how I throw?"

"You betcha. That guy probably shit his pants. Your house is, more than likely, the safest from human invasion now." He pulled her into a hug.

She stood silent.

"I'm glad you're safe. Do you want to show me that knife you took from him, now?" Caine asked in his smoothest voice.

"Sure." Ava walked upstairs, retrieved the knife, and brought it to Caine.

"This is interesting. It seems to be one of the knives stolen from the nest when they were raided." Caine was spinning the tip of it against his index finger pad.

"Was that a Hunter?" She gasped.

"No, a true Hunter would have killed you without hesitation. It was probably just some unlucky human." Caine chuckled while he thought about her aim.

"Oh." She slumped into her chair.

"Ava, are you okay? You look a little pale." He was watching her intently.

Her eyes were withdrawn. The night had obviously taken a toll on her. Caine stood up and let his weakness for the half-breed female show. Caine felt drawn to her out of his duty to Avaraz, his weakened friend, he attempted to rationalize as he reached around Ava's small body and picked her up. She seemed alarmed when his arms went under her as he scooped her up.

"What…" she started to protest.

"You need rest. I am taking you to bed." He listened as her heart thudded a bit louder than before.

"You don't need to carry me," she protested again. She always liked to seem in control. Interesting.

"I do need to because I do not trust that your knees won't give out if you attempt to take these stairs on your own." He adjusted her weight in his arms and continued to walk. He took the stairs easily, and his breathing did not even change.

Caine walked through the kicked-down door. He already knew it happened, but seeing it firsthand made his blood boil with the full fury of his warrior heritage. The urge to kill, to protect his kind from a senseless attack, burned within him. The only thing that prevented him from leaving was Ava's soft hand on his shirt. She needed him more than she would admit, not that he wanted her to need him or want him.

"What's wrong?" she asked. Her violet eyes locked on his. An odd concern was in them.

"I'm just angry, Ava. Someone is hunting the demon kind to damn near extinction, and then measly humans are invading your home. It's a lot to think about." He set her in the big bed in front of him.

"Oh," she said slowly.

"Yes, I just came from a meeting with the elders of our faction. It is unclear how the Hunters received their information. We are going through our ranks."

She yawned wide, and her eyes fluttered closed. She spoke with the softness of being in a dream, "What if there is a traitor?"

Her breathing got deeper. He chuckled before answering. Caine was sure she was already asleep. "Then, we kill the traitor to protect our kind."

"Oh," was all she could manage.

Sleep took over her body. She relaxed and fell deeper into sleep. Her pulse and respiration slowed. Caine stood from her bed and walked to her door.

Using a variation of a glamour spell, he waved his hand in front of the door. The pieces began to bond back together and affix themselves to the hinges.

Caine walked downstairs and did the same to the door in the main entry. He was uneasy about leaving Ava alone once more. Since he was already using magic on the house, he decided to seal the door so no magical entity could enter. He then set about fixing the lock to make it harder to break in, just in case the masked visitor returned.

He shimmered off after one last check on Ava, who was lightly snoring. Caine was going to torture her about that. Perhaps, even jest that it was a water buffalo sound.

The wall had become increasingly heavy over the last week. At least, Avaraz estimated it had been a week. There were only so many times you could count to a trillion and not go insane from the repetition. Caine would be coming soon. He had to hold on. Maybe Caine had figured something out about his daughter. Perhaps, it was silly that Avaraz still held on, that he thought he deserved anything good in his life. After all, he was a demon.

Magic shimmered a few feet away and soon Caine was standing before Avaraz. He looked almost worried.

"My old friend, what troubles you?" Avaraz spoke.

"You are the one bearing punishment, yet you worry for me. You are misguided, my friend." Caine chuckled and went closer to Avaraz's confinement chains.

"Is there trouble on earth?" He had to question him and ask after his daughter.

"Your offspring is fine. There was trouble this evening with a mortal, but the issue resolved itself." Caine's smile both intrigued and worried Avaraz.

"What happened?" the worried father won out.

"A human broke into her house. She actually threw quite a powerful energy ball at the intruder. I am very impressed," Caine reassured him that it was nothing to do with sex. Demons of lust could be indiscriminate, and he wanted more for his daughter.

"She used her magic?" Avaraz pulled at his restraints, then hissed at the pain, which came swiftly, following his actions.

"Yes, that is what we are wanting, right? She is a natural. I think she will be ready for war soon." Caine's smile was triumphant, but it broke Avaraz's heart.

"I did not want her brought into this fight. It is not hers to bear." A thousand years of sorrow sounded in his tone.

"She was born as one of us. She should live as one of us," Caine defended his decision.

"She will be trapped, unable to live normally. Who will she love? Who will she trust after she sees what happens here?" Avaraz's voice became stronger.

"I do not think she will survive if she does not know everything and come for training. She needs to know the truth, my friend," Caine continued.

"She is not supposed to die as a demon," Avaraz growled.

"Should I stop her training?" he suggested a possible solution.

"No, the fact that she has connected to her powers is a concern. The magic concealing her location and her identity from hunters and other demons will soon be deteriorated completely. She will be left in the open. You have brought her out of hiding. You will train her, and continue to protect her better than you have thus far," Avaraz set his terms. He could see into Caine's head easily. He did not need contact to read thoughts. His senses were honed even after years of infrequent use.

"Yes, my friend. I will do my best," Caine promised. He bowed his head and brought his fist to his heart, pledging his honor.

Avaraz hoped he was serious. The most precious possession he had never held was now in Caine's care.

CHAPTER 6

Her back hit the ground hard once more. After the thud echoed in the room, Ava's dismayed 'oof' sounded. She was panting like a dog.

"Enough for today." Ava attempted to demand a break; Caine offered his hand to help her up.

"Do you think our enemies will give you a time out if you're tired?" he snapped.

"No," her tone was clipped, "I want to know more about the magic that protected my house. How long will it work?" She was concerned for her uncle.

"It is fading fast. You have been accessing your powers. But the biggest hit to the structure of the protection magic was the fact that you used your powers in the house against someone."

"Shit. Is Isaac in danger?" She leapt up as if she were going to shimmer home to protect him.

"Calm yourself, Ava. He is fine. The magic is weakened, yes, but it will only be destroyed when you make your first kill."

"Kill?" she croaked the word.

"Yes, you will have to kill, or do you think you'll get away with showing off your breasts and saying please?" Caine teased her. She grinned at the banter.

"You've looked at my breasts?" It was her turn to make him squirm.

"Yes, I am a demon of lust. Of course, I looked. You have a body built for sex. Most of us do. You exude a certain sexual power." He shrugged. It would be impossible to make him blush.

"Oh." She covered her sports bra with her arms.

"We can be done for now. You can get your education in. We need to work on your powers." He was business as usual again.

"You're so collected. Is that part of learning how to control your powers?" she asked.

"Yes, you need to be able to control your anger, sorrow, happiness, and more. Without control, you will not survive." Caine nodded and he walked behind her. His hands went to her shoulders.

"What are you doing?" She tried to turn, but he held her in place.

"Shh, you must relax. You need to gather yourself and remain calm. I want you to shimmer." His fingers began to move and massage her.

"Ohh." Her sound was guttural and pleasured.

"That's it. Relax. Let loose," he whispered into her ear. His lips caressed her earlobe.

Ava's body trembled lightly, but she tried to concentrate on the task at hand. She closed her eyes and listened harder to his words. She needed to relax, and imagine completing her task. She took a deep steadying breath and held onto the feeling in the pit of her stomach. It started to grow. She could feel the air around her charge with the magic from within her body. She was starting to prepare. Ava kept her surprise in check. She dug deeper and the air felt different. The magic was growing.

Caine let go of her shoulders and the magic built around her. Moments later, she visualized where she wanted to go. She saw outside the doors of the rundown factory she was in. She saw the river that sounded in the background. Then, the magic cloaked her body and she was lifted. Ava felt the particles that were her soar, leaving a musky smell behind. She took another breath and the air was fresher. She opened her eyes and she was standing on the patch of manicured grass outside. Caine shimmered beside her.

"Good girl." He wrapped his massive arms around her.

"I DID IT!"

"Yes, yes you did." He laughed low and removed himself from the quick hug.

"This is the first big progress I can see." She was beaming.

"If you can shimmer back inside, you can leave early. I do not want to use all your energy so fast. You need to relax." He nodded.

"Plus, I need to go to school." She further stated.

"Why are you still playing human?" He was uneasy and that was simple to tell.

"I am almost done with my degree. Even if I have all these powers, why can't I stay in school? I want to be well educated. It's a piece of paper with my name and I want to know I can do it." Her voice was a little more emotional. There was more than that one reason, but Caine did not need to know.

"I see." He let the conversation be and shimmered inside.

Ava had to concentrate still. The magic came easier this time, and she was back inside next to the bench where she set her bag, just a moment later. She was proud of herself. Her triumphant smile returned. Maybe she would make a good demon after all?

Michael waited outside the main entrance to the building. His mind was sorting every detail and scenario on what he could say. He had reacted badly, so badly that Ava hadn't contacted him nor had she been to class. Michael sat every day in front until the last possible minute. He hoped to catch Ava walking in, but each day was a failure. Finally he saw it, her cute little red Honda. He stood up and straightened his clothing out. Michael wanted to make sure his ass wasn't numb when he tried to walk to her. How would he begin his groveling? Should he go right for the get-on-his-knees style? Should he play it at least a little cool? He wanted to ask her a few things and he needed to get her away from her uncle and whomever else she may have been hanging around with.

"Ava!" He waved at her and took off at a slow jog.

She froze mid-step. She almost missed the curb, but somehow caught herself. It seemed she had been learning to be more graceful during her time away from school.

"Where have you been, beautiful?" he tried flattery first.

"I've been busy with a family emergency. I called our professor and told him." She was not trying to look at him. Instead, she was digging in her bag.

"Here." She handed him a portfolio. He accepted it and looked through it.

"You've been busy." He noted and saw it was the majority of their project done, all of her parts, plus a few of his.

"Yeah, I didn't want you showing up at my house again unannounced." Her tone was icy.

"Sorry about that..." he trailed off, rubbing the back of his neck.

"You should be." Ava was very stubborn and wouldn't let up.

"Come on, Ava, I really am sorry." He gave his best contrite look.

"I accept your apology," she said on a sigh.

"Excellent. Now, how about to prove how sorry I am and I take you on a date tonight?" he asked, not being quite subtle.

"I don't know.".

"I promise to behave. You don't even have to kiss me goodnight." He tried his best dazzling smile.

"Fine, can we go to class now, or do you want me to miss another day?" She shot him a knowing look.

"Let's go." He offered her his arm, but she walked past it. He knew she would. She was a very independent little female.

Michael walked Ava into their class and they sat in their usual spots. This time, he took the chance to put his arm around her. It was a slightly possessive move. He always wondered what sort of man she liked. She was always reading those romance novels, so he had to imagine she liked the more domineering man who was in touch with his sensitive side as well. Hell, he could at least pretend to be what she needed. Maybe he could be, but it was a long shot. Life wasn't designed to have a happy ending.

After class, Ava and Michael agreed to the details of their date and she went home, Michael was supposed to meet her at the restaurant in three hours.

She wanted to be able to get ready leisurely. The silence in the house seemed to scream at her. Since she had been wearing a lot of sweat pants and jeans, Ava opted for a dress and heels over her now normal attire. Her hair was in curlers when the air shimmered behind her in the bathroom, and suddenly Caine filled the space behind her. A small yelp escaped her lips and she tightened her robe to prevent him from seeing her undergarments.

"Do you knock?" she chastised him.

"Why are you dressing up?" He looked confused.

"I am taking the night off from training, so I can be normal." She went back to fixing her lip-gloss. She could feel Caine's anger. When she glanced up, the look on his face was conflicted.

"You are not normal, Ava. You are not just human. You are also like me." He didn't say demon this time.

"I can be somewhat normal until I kill someone, right? I just want one night off to go on a date." She said the words aloud and felt as if she were betraying him. Guilt overwhelmed her.

"What?" He caught her stare in the mirror.

"I... I wanted to go out on a date with a classmate. It is just a stupid way for him to apologize for putting his hands on me." The second they left her lips she wanted to grab them back.

"HE DID WHAT?" Caine growled and grew with his anger. He dwarfed Ava with his fury.

"That's not what I meant. He just grabbed my arm. He was mad at me for missing class." She tried to make excuses for Michael's bad behavior.

"Did he, without permission, put his hands on your flesh?" Caine asked.

"Yes." There was no way around that direct line of questioning.

"Did you tell him to let go?" Caine probed further.

"Yes." She could feel her teeth grinding in her mouth.

"That is a high offense, punishable by death." Caine flexed his fingers in and out of a fist.

"Stop it, Caine. Shit happens to humans. If he tries his shit again, I'll put him on his ass. You can stop that over protective crap. I won't be put in a bubble. You are bringing me into a war with creatures I didn't even know existed until recently. The least you can do, is give me one night of normal." Ava ranted, punctuating her point with sharp shoves to his shoulder, which did practically nothing, except make her feel better.

"Fine." Caine turned her own word against her.

"Thank you," she said. His eyes showed a shimmer of something.

"What are you wearing?" Caine seemed to be interested.

"The black dress on my bed," she said casually. Caine walked out of the bathroom and to her bedroom. She felt her body heat.

How many times had she imagined Caine in her bedroom since they met? Thousands. He probably knew each little fantasy she had about him. The thought he knew made her bite her lip. He knew. Why else would he have such a willingness to go to her bedroom?

"Are you sure you should wear a dress? It's turning cold out," Caine expressed some concern, and Ava had to smile.

"I will be fine. I will be in my car, then the restaurant, then back again." She hoped that he knew she wouldn't be going home with Michael.

"I see." He gazed around her room, as if he wanted to memorize it.

"Yeah." She let the conversation ebb.

"Why are you going out with this human? Even if you like him and it worked out, you would never be permitted to be with him." Caine was obvious in his anger.

"I just want to be normal. Michael is more of a buddy to me. This is his way of apologizing. Free food." She shrugged and sat on her bed, worrying the edge of her favorite blanket.

"Demons are not to mate with humans unless they want the human killed or turned into a demon," he repeated his intent.

"Why are you so pushy about my love life, Caine?" She looked up at him with questioning eyes.

"I just want to be sure you know the consequences of your actions, Ava." He growled. His lip even picked up in a bit of a snarl.

"Stop your shit. You're hot and cold. You kiss me like I've never been kissed, then act like you want to throw me off the Empire State Building!" she shot at him.

Caine stood there in silence, which made Ava persist. She was pissed.

"Are you jealous or something? Or are you just a bitter old demon?" She pushed past him.

"I'm just warning you, child." He knew how much she hated that word. Before she could turn on him and express exactly how deep her hatred was for that word, he shimmered out.

"COWARD!" she yelled at thin air. She didn't know if he would hear it, but it made her feel better.

Caine had to leave the room. He used the word she loathed, and one thing you did not do, was piss off a female demon. They were some of the most vindictive creatures ever created. He did not leave the house. The jealousy he felt ringing through his veins made it impossible to leave.

He was jealous. He was jealous of some mortal taking Ava out, or was he just angry that she was skipping her training? He didn't know. He couldn't say. The fire he felt when she poked him was strange. It must have been her powers manifesting due to her internal fire. He had to rationalize it in his mind. There was no way it was true jealousy over a human he could snap in a moment. There was no competition.

His ears perked when she yelled out, calling him a coward. Was he? No, she was just mad that he got the last word. He chuckled darkly from his hiding spot. He kept tabs on her movements through the house. When she dressed, he watched her beautiful form twist and wriggle into the clothing. The dress was a second skin and looked just as good as bare flesh, almost.

She continued to prepare for her date, and when she was ready, she picked up her phone. Caine slipped into her mind gently to keep it from being noticed. There was hesitation in her heart as she spoke to the other male.

"Yes, I am just about to leave, Michael," she gave him the soft placating tone.

"You just bring your beautiful face and your appetite. The rest is on me, baby girl." He was overly familiar with her and that grated on Caine's nerves.

"Yeah, yeah, yeah. I'll see you in a few minutes," she countered.

"I'll be waiting for you, Ava." He sounded somewhat hopeful.

"See you." She hung up and started looking for her pea coat that would cover her entire dress.

Ava finished getting ready and checked her mirror before she walked out, locking the door behind her. Caine stepped from his hiding spot and watched her go to her car. He wasn't sure what he was going to do, or why. All he knew was that Ava was too important to let her go on this "date" without his kind of chaperoning.

After Caine's departure and the phone call, Ava felt somewhat odd leaving. She primped and checked her lips before heading out the door. Caine had pissed her off. She had to shake off what he did. It was most likely some sort of control lesson. If he wanted to see control, she would show it to him. Tonight, she would be normal for the first time in what felt like years, already. She would be normal and enjoy a night out, even if it was just a friend apologizing for what he did.

She pulled up to the restaurant and went inside. There he was. Michael was waiting, and he looked dapper in his suit top, button down shirt, and dark wash jeans. He was handsome. He was facing toward the bar, shifting from left to right. Ava removed her jacket and hung it over her arm, adjusting the hem of her dress slightly. When Michael finally turned around, she was back in stride and walking toward him. The surprise on his face was a good reaction. At least, to her it seemed like one. He looked her up and down several times, gulping hard.

"Hey." She smiled at him.

"Wow, Ava…wow." He was rendered speechless. That had to be a good thing, right? "Is this okay?" She wiped down the front of her dress with her free hand.

"Yeah, you're just going to be breaking the heart of every man here; except for me, of course." He turned into his cocky self.

"I see." She chuckled softly.

"Come on. Our table is ready." A goofy grin crossed his face and Ava had to follow suit. Happy Michael was the one she knew and liked.

She followed him to the table in the corner of the small Mexican restaurant. It was a gem of the city. Not too many people knew about it, but the food was wonderful. Michael pulled out the chair for Ava to sit. She smiled and took her spot.

Michael sat across from her, looking nervous. Even from this distance, she could tell his hands were sweaty. It was sort of cute; maybe even endearing that he was so nervous around her.

"So, am I done being punished?" He asked sheepishly.

"I haven't decided yet." She smirked. The waiter placed a fresh basket of tortilla chips between them. Ava picked one chip up and dipped it into the salsa.

Michael watched her while she ate the chip. When she noticed he was watching, she became self-conscious about it and covered her mouth. "What?" she asked.

"I am just watching you eat. It's very sexy." He grinned at her.

"Hmm, so you know why you are in trouble, right?" She put her napkin onto her lap and began looking over the leather-bound menu.

"Yes, I crossed the line. I fucked up." He reached for her hand.

"Why are you doing that?" She let him pick it up.

"I want to apologize again. I was drinking that night, and I should not have come to your house. I missed you, but there were better ways to take care of that. I can't ever express enough how sorry I am to have done that to you." He was staring right in her eyes and stroking the back of her hand lightly with his fingers.

"You weren't the worst thing I dealt with this week." She gave a sly grin.

"Oh, what was the worst?" he asked.

"Someone broke into my house, attempted to rob me and probably kill me. Something scared him off, luckily." She sipped her water.

Michael stiffened. "Are you okay? Do you want me to come stay with you?"

"No, I'm fine. I promise. My uncle will be back soon." She shifted, uncomfortable with the thought of him staying near her.

"You sure?" Ava had to hide her laugh from his poor attemptto sound alluring and.

"Yes, I am sure."

That was a temporary end to the conversation because the waiter appeared to take their order. He said it would be right up and disappeared, leaving them alone again. Ava would have to make some sort of conversation.

The kid was attempting to be suave. Caine watched every nuance of his face. He liked Ava a lot. The thought alone made Caine itchy. There was something about this Michael kid that made Caine feel uneasy. He held himself differently than others would. He seemed assured of his success. He was very prideful. Caine hated that the scent of demonic power was rolling off of him. Ava had spent time with him earlier in the day, and was doing so again now. She seemed to be taken in by his human charms.

Caine stayed in the darkness, shrouded by his powers. The kid scanned the room several times while they sat and talked. Their order came quickly to Caine's relief. It was much safer for Ava to be where he could protect her as he had done every night that he wasn't in the pit giving her father an update on her progress. The out in the open stuff was not good for his nerves. There could be an attack from any direction. He scanned again.

Michael was a ball of nerves. Ava was gorgeous, and her violet eyes otherworldly. He felt like she could stare right down into the depth of his soul and see every secret he possessed. They ate in relative silence. He was trying to figure out how to make conversation. The home invasion was something that he did not want to continue talking about. He took their silence to think of different topics.

"So, where have you been? Class has been quiet without you." He figured that subject was safe.

"I've been doing research on my family history. I guess time got away from me." She tried to shrug it off.

He sensed it was a lie to cover up something she was hiding. Michael wanted to dig further. "What about your family?"

"Information on my father," she said casually.

"What about him?" he pressed.

"Just information on him, I'm talking to old friends of his. I want to know about him. He's half of who I am."

"I can dig it." Michael laughed and reached for Ava's hands again after they finished their meal.

Ava felt awkward throughout the date. They glossed over the project details and delved into other subjects. She contained herself easily. She did not feel the fire burn when she was near him. Her body did not betray her. It was difficult to keep her mind from wandering to Caine. She did enjoy Michael's company, but not as much as she enjoyed Caine's. The end of the date was coming fast. Her mind played out different scenarios, each more unpleasant than the last.

Ava moved her hands back whenever he reached for them. She didn't wish Michael to read too much into the date. It would be unfair for him to think there was a chance for more, when there wasn't. She wanted

Caine, even if it was foolish of her to want him how she did. She made up an excuse.

"I have an early morning tomorrow. I have to hit the gym and then go work at my uncle's store," she said smoothly. Lying was regretfully becoming second nature to her.

"I see," he said.

"I had a lot of fun, though," she tacked on.

"You did?" Michael perked up.

"Yeah." Ava watched the waitress drop the check off and Michael paid it quickly.

She stood and pushed her own chair out, as she didn't think it would be wise to wait for him to pull it out for her. She was not a damsel in distress; she pulled on her jacket and attempted to keep her sigh to herself. Michael tried to wrap his hand around her waist when they walked outside, but she sidestepped to avoid it. He walked her to her car, and the awkward tension seemed to rise the closer they got to her driver side door.

"You look beautiful." He reached up to her hair and pushed the free strands behind her ear.

She shrunk away from his touch. Again, he seemed to be reading into the date. She was almost nauseated by how close he was attempting to be.

"Michael." Her voice was a warning he did not heed.

Caine could not believe his eyes. Even more shocking was his reaction. He hated the other male being near Ava. It was surprisingly difficult for him. Michael, as she called him, had his hands on her at every turn. He was being physical with her and he wanted her. It was obvious. The scent that was thrown off by him was arousal and desire. Caine stayed hidden in the shadows. Ava did not need to know he was there, essentially spying on her and her date. Caine just couldn't shake the feeling that he could not trust her friend, Michael, especially after his hands were on her.

He loomed closer as they walked toward her car. His eyes scanned every movement, and his ears picked up every word. Caine bit his tongue hard when Michael had Ava trapped against the door of her car. Caine moved even closer.

"Michael." He heard Ava's voice. It was breathy, distant, and almost scared.

Ava's date seemed not to notice every negative nuance of her body language and her voice. Michael moved in closer and closer. Ava tried to put her hands up to stop him. They were against his chest. She was saying, "No, do not kiss me."

Then it happened, and Caine's world seemed to stop as he waited for her reaction. He kissed her. Michael kissed Ava. His lips moved against hers, seeking her reaction. Caine's lips peeled back from his teeth and he surprised himself with a snarl. He watched every muscle in both of their bodies. Her body stayed taut with tension. She pressed her hands into his chest and pushed him back.

"Michael, I said no," she protested.

"You didn't mean it." He moved back closer to her and brought his lips down to her slender neck.

She shoved him harder this time. "Michael, I don't like you that way." Her voice was stern, yet still caring, like she was a parent scolding a naughty child.

"I know you want me, Ava. The way you looked tonight couldn't have been an accident. You are absolutely scrumptious," he countered.

Ava did look beautiful. She had to know the allure she held. She could bend any man to her will, even Caine. It was not just her looks. It was her heart, the purity of her thoughts, and her soul. "I didn't mean for this to get your hopes up, Michael, but read my lips. *WE ARE NOT COMPATIBLE*," she growled, accenting every word to be sure he understood.

"Yes, we are. You just have to let down your guard." He pressed his body closer to her.

Caine took a step forward, ready to reveal his slightly stalker tendencies to Ava, and introduce his fist to Michael's face, but Ava took to the offensive.

"I have let my guard down and it isn't with you, Michael. You are my friend. I do not want you romantically." She pressed her finger into his chest and backed him up.

"You don't need him, you have me, Ava. I've been here longer. I've wanted you to join me since I first met you."

"Michael, you're forgetting. We're buddies, not dating. Please stop trying this. I knew this date was a bad idea." She opened her car door and turned to get in.

Caine was impressed. She handled him like a lady. She was nearly safe, so Caine took a step back. He would shimmer to her home and surprise her with his own admission to her this time, since she could admit her preference of him to the other. She was choosing Caine and that made him oddly happy.

The moment he turned around, Caine heard something he wished he hadn't. Michael mumbled the word "bitch."

Caine whirled around just in time to watch Ava's fist curl at her side, the energy was flowing fast. She was too angry to contain her powers and this would not end well.

Ava saw the word forming on Michael's lips. The brazen bastard was stupid enough to mumble it in front of her. Michael called her a bitch. Before she knew it, her fist was curled and there was no stopping her. Her fist flew forward as if she did not control it. At the last second, she noticed the energy surrounding it. Her left fist connected hard with his jaw. She could feel her eyes flash a brutal red.

"I am not a bitch just because I won't fuck you, Michael." He looked her square in the eyes now. A heated glare was exchanged between the two.

She continued, "I am turning in my portion of the project tomorrow, and you will not contact me again. I never want to see you or hear from you. You are nothing but a child throwing a fit, and I have no time for children in my life. I have far too much to worry about, without having to think about damaging your little ego." She looked pointedly at his crotch, which he had been rubbing against her moments ago.

"The man I prefer over you would never call me that." She let that hang in the air as she got in her car and sped off toward her home.

Caine had to resist the urge to follow up with Michael and teach him manners about women, just in case he did not learn his lesson from the intense blow Ava just delivered to his jaw. It served him right. You don't mess with a strong female, especially one that had demonic blood. Those ones loved to fight.

He simply chuckled in the darkness and shimmered to Ava's house, after making one quick stop on the way.

CHAPTER 7

Caine's errand proved to be nearly futile. The small shop had nothing he needed to start his unexpected wooing of Ava. She had denied the other male vying for her attention. She had to have some sort of interest in him. Caine had to stop on his way out of the small bodega style shop and look at his reflection in the glass. Who was he? He was practically fawning over a half-breed. Ava had come into his life on a whim, and now he was aching to make it more permanent. Perhaps that is why he defied Avaraz. He shook his head. It was sexual. It had to be just sexual need for him. Demons, lust demons in particular, seldom held any sort of mating status.

The second he was alone and able to shimmer, he did so. He was back inside her home. The scent hit him like a ton of bricks. She wasn't home, yet her

133

natural scent lingered. He could pinpoint it in a crowd if he needed to. Fuck. He needed to get laid. If he wasn't careful, he was going to cross the line. Caine decided to throw away the cheap candy and bouquet of nearly wilting roses he had bought. It would be inappropriate if he pushed Ava into something he wanted. She was young and human, and she would have read too much into the small gesture.

Ava parked her car and went inside the house. She kicked off her shoes at the door, left them there, and went straight for the liquor cabinet in the kitchen. She flipped on the light without looking around, and took out the bottle of high priced vodka and proceeded to pour herself a large glass. After she took the first burning sip of it, she cradled it against her chest and cursed her stupidity for even accepting the date with Michael. She knew in the back of her mind, she would be giving him hope where he had none.

"Did you have a good date?" Caine asked suddenly.

She nearly jumped out of her skin. Her body wheeled around and she reached out to slap him, but he was across the room. "Damn it, Caine. You scared me!" She glared. She didn't need the emotional mind fuck again.

"Did you?" He asked again, remaining in his seat.

"Not that you have dibs on every night of mine, and not that it is your business, but no, I didn't have a good time." She took another long drink from her glass.

"Please, remember not to get too drunk tonight. You have training again tomorrow." He nodded toward the clock.

"Oh, yes, master, I will remember." Her voice was dry and sarcastic.

"Good girl." He chose a praise that would be used for a dog as his parting words for her.

At least he was smart enough to disappear again when he uttered them. Ava had begun to advance on him as he shimmered away. Now, Ava was angry, frustrated, and had the scent of Caine in her nose. It was going to be another long night for her.

She grumbled and refilled her glass before she went to her room to boot up her computer. Michael had already left several messages on her chat box, cell phone, email, voicemail, and any social media he could find her on. Each one was more groveling and pathetic than the last. Then he started to become frantic, and finally, he got angry. She deleted each before it even ended. She was done attempting to be his friend. No one called her a bitch, put hands on her, and stayed in her life the three did not mix.

She huffed loudly and went to her student email to message the professor that her and Michael had quite the argument and would be finishing the project separately. She gave the details of the final straw, attached her files, and hit send. The moment she was pinged that her message was sent, she felt relief flood her body. It was as if the weight disappeared completely. She still had demon training left, but it would be easier without a final project looming over her shoulders for the next few weeks. Sometimes, it was good to be an overachiever.

When Ava was finished with her drink, she went back to the kitchen to wash her glass. After she finished drying it, she opened the trashcan with her foot and saw inside.

"What the?" she mumbled.

She reached in and pulled out blood red roses and her favorite candy bar. Chocolate did sound good, but she would not be eating it out of the trashcan. She dropped the chocolate back in and looked at the flowers, no tag. Caine was the only one who had been inside her home that she knew of, unless the person who broke in wanted to apologize to her...

Ava let the flowers fall back into the trash. Why would Caine get her flowers? Was that going to be his way of apologizing to her for his raucous behavior? He would need to do a lot more than that to win her over to the dark side. A small chuckle escaped her mouth at her thought of being a demon and the dark side. She was already a part of the dark side. Caine was just going to drag her deeper. If he could act like a gentleman toward her, perhaps she would let him drag her further into it. Maybe.

Dawn came too fast for Ava. It seemed her mind finally let her fall into a peaceful sleep when her cell phone began to sound its deafening alarm to wake her up. She groaned loudly, "Demon training, why does it have to start so damn early? Why couldn't demons be night owls?" She lamented while she brushed her teeth and prepared for the day.

Instead of her usual walking route, she decided to shimmer around her home. She could see becoming too lazy to walk, if she could master her ability. A thrill of excitement shot through her. No more having to find parking at school, or anywhere in New York. She marked an imaginary score board with a winning score. Her biggest test was yet to come. Once she was ready and strapped with the weapons that Caine supplied her with, she closed her eyes and began to concentrate. She envisioned the entire journey to the facility. She felt the magic in the air begin to morph as she pulled it into herself and shimmered the great distance.

The surprise was plain on Caine's face when she was suddenly in the training room. Her grin was one of self-satisfaction. Ava walked to the bench and put her bag down, taking things out of it without a word.

"Did you shimmer from your home?" Caine asked.

"Yes." Ava was still trying to decipher the chocolate and flowers.

"Listen, about last night…" he began.

"Not going there today, Caine," she interrupted him with one finger in the air she obviously meant business.

"Then, let's get to training."

Ava's interjection interrupted him. Caine was used to being the dominating one in conversations. He did not like the idea she had become so comfortable with him, her casual feeling was exemplified when she walked around seemingly ignoring the fact he was standing near. The fact he would not use his powers against her, allowed her to believe that she could. He suppressed a grumble, stood to his full height and walked up behind her. When her eyes bugged out from surprise, he smirked. He still had it. His irritation dissipated slightly.

"What are we doing today?" She gulped loud enough for him to hear.

"Mental blocking," he stated with a smirk, this was one he was going to enjoy.

"Mental Blocking?" she echoed with an upward inflection.

"Yes, you need to learn to block others from getting into your mind. What you possess is very valuable. You need to keep strong mental blocks from other demons. They will use what you have to hurt the collective. As a seer, you will have the most danger," he explained.

"I see. So, how do I do that?" she asked.

"You just have to lock your brain. There are some who can read past and present thoughts. Your father can see futures, too. I believe you have some of the same tendencies." He praised her father greatly, and Avaraz deserved it.

"How do I lock my mind?" she asked again.

"Imagine it locked. You stop projecting, concentrate on your thoughts and push them deep inside," he explained the best he could.

"Okay, now how do I know if it worked?"

"That's where I come in." He smirked sadistically.

"I don't feel anything." she said.

"I haven't started yet."

"Oh." She blushed.

Caine let her one word hang in the air between them. He kept his red eyes on her form and let his mind reach out to gently caress hers. She flinched. She felt him inside her mind.

"Fight back, Ava. Force me out." He delved deeper into her mind.

"I'm trying." She gritted her teeth.

"Try harder." He was accessing memories. He let her see which ones he was looking at.

Caine saw the memory of the night he came out to her as a demon. She hadn't believed him. When he saw how she reacted at the thought she tried to squash, he went deeper. In her memory, she held each sensation of her hands as she imagined his would be on her. She kept trying to push him back. For a moment, it worked, but he overpowered her and wanted to see the memory of her fingers caressing her female flesh. Caine licked his lips and stopped for a second. She was whimpering from the pressure he was putting on her mind.

"The enemies will not let up," he noted while her chest heaved for air.

"I'm trying." She was glaring at him again.

"You were having quite a good time with me in your memory." A dark chuckle came from his throat.

"That was before I knew you were this annoying," she was quick with her reply.

"Do you want me to touch you, Ava?" he whispered in her ear, his lips caressing her lobe. He felt her knees wobble.

"No," she shot back. Her mouth said one thing, but her body said the other.

"Then, keep me away from your memories. Others will use them against you," he ordered.

"Fine, again."

He pushed his influence into her mind for hours upon hours after their last banter session. The mental exertion proved to be intense. Ava was covered in a heavy sheen of sweat as they stood frozen, one battling to get in, the other battling to keep him out. She panted and pushed him out successfully. Caine was pleasantly surprised for the second time, when she succeeded at keeping him at bay.

"You have done wonderful for your first try," he complimented her. The words sounded awkward coming from his mouth.

"Thank you." She took a long pull at her water bottle. He couldn't help but watch her chest.

"Your memories are quite vivid." He sat down to hide his erection from her.

"Yeah…" she trailed off.

"Ava, I am a friend of your father's, and I made certain promises to him," Caine attempted to explain.

"What sort of promises?" She shot him a look. She attempted to keep her cool around him, even though her blood pressure picked up slightly.

"Ones I had every intention of keeping, but I won't." He dropped the towel he was wiping his face with and started moving toward her.

His movements were lithe, like a panther stalking its prey. She was in his sights and he was going to let her know exactly how much he desired her. Something in his mind had snapped. He had to give into the desire.

"What?"

"I cannot keep the promise to leave your virtue untainted by a demon." He looked right into her eyes. The violet color burned into him. If she denied him, he would never forget the look.

"What?" she repeated.

His eyes scorched her. The red seemed to flame as he got closer to her. She was fumbling over words in her head. Ava was lost. She wanted him, and after the multiple memories he found that he had starred in she couldn't deny that she wanted him.

"I have tried to deny, quantify, and change what I thought of you, Ava, and I cannot. You are a beautiful woman. Half-breed or not, I want to have you." His hand softly brushed through her hair, fisting part behind her head.

"If you say no, it will ruin me, but I will listen," he continued.

She said nothing. Her eyes fluttered, but she remained speechless. Caine's warm lips touched hers, once, gently. He was swooping over her mouth, as if testing how far he could push her. It was as soft and tender as a dream. Her libido began to shoot through the roof. She wanted to pull him, push him, bring him to her, scrape him, bite his lips, and much more. She tried to quell the animalistic need that coursed through her veins as his lips slowly covered hers over and over. Ava pushed against Caine's chest, their lips separated for a moment, but his eyes were still locked on hers.

"Is that a refusal?" he asked.

"No, it's just... I don't understand. You're so confusing. You keep saying I'm not your type. You don't want me, and then all of a sudden you *do* want me. You're giving me whiplash," she griped, but all she wanted to do was undress him.

"I was trying to respect your father. Ava, I know you want me as much as I want you. I do not wish to fight it. I will suffer whatever consequences I must, but I want to taste every part of your beautiful flesh." His voice was husky and full of so much promise.

"I do want you," she tacked on confirmation of what he knew without a doubt already.

His smile was triumphant. Caine moved back in close to her and each of his hands wrapped around her hips and pulled her against his massive chest. Ava's fingers clutched to his workout shirt, fisting it in her hands. The control she was attempting to exhibit was slipping fast.

"You are beautiful, Ava." His words were as gentle as a lover's should be.

Her only reply was a soft moan.

When the audible moan came into his ear he gripped her hips tighter and covered her mouth once more. This time his lips were heavier, full of the need they both felt. Caine was becoming extremely greedy, the more he had of her the more he wanted. One hand went to her perfectly round backside and pressed her into him. A small gasp escaped her lips when she felt the bulge that ached for her approval.

Another moan sounded softly from her throat and he took the opening of her mouth to let his tongue slip in and taste her sweet lips deeper. One of Caine's hands stayed on her hip, the other that was on her ass brought her closer still and lifted her up. Ava's legs wrapped around Caine's hips. He held her easily and walked to the closest wall he could find and leaned her body against it, he had her pinned with his body and he had never felt more elated. A soft entry into her mind showed that she had not either, but the memory of another lover did not please Caine. At least the lover was long ago.

He was determined to make her completely forget about the previous suitors who had won her attention. He rolled his tongue against her lips, a tempting tease of what was to come. What he intended to only be a kiss was morphing into something much more powerful. Caine swiveled his hips and ground his groin into her. Another beautiful moan echoed in the empty training center. She wrapped her delicate arms around his neck.

"Take your shirt off, please. I want to feel your skin." Ava was so ballsy at times, and timid at others, Caine was surprised yet again.

"Your wish is my command." He took her hands in his and pulled up his shirt, Caine let Ava explore his abs and chest as he slowly pulled off his shirt revealing tattoos, scars, and the muscles she fantasized about.

Her supple mouth leaned closer to him and traced the column of his neck. It was Caine's turn to bark out a moan of Ava's name. Her tongue ventured from between her lips and she teased his skin. He resisted the urge to go into her mind and push her pleasure; he wanted to learn what drove her crazy sexually the old fashioned way. It would be fun for him.

When her lips suckled on the bottom of his ear lobe his cock jumped and demanded attention. Caine's powerful hips flexed and pressed against Ava's frame. She tilted them and Caine almost mutilated his clothes in an attempt to get them off. There was no stopping his carnal need.

Time and time again, Ava felt the bulge of his manhood push against her. He was very large between the legs – just as he was everywhere else. Ava's core was begging and weeping. She continued to kiss, and added in bites. He seemed to react strongest when she bit his neck and then his lower lip. Each time he would push his hips up into hers harder. It was enough to drive her crazy. She bit at his lip again and tugged, another moan. She liked feeling like a demonic sexual goddess and he was definitely making her feel that way. His approval sated her. She gained pleasure from his pleasure.

Ava was putty in Caine's hands. She suspected he was putty in hers, as well. Her arms left his neck and reached between them, she pushed his athletic shorts down as much as she could then looked into his eyes. They were burning into her again. His mouth attacked hers once more. Their mouths were moving in a frenzy. He pulled at her clothes and when he became frustrated he gripped the fabric in his hands and pulled, he tore her shorts to shreds, but left her panties intact.

She whimpered and ground her nearly naked body against his again, she was too deep in need to be coherent.

"Patience, my Ava. I will remove those." He sat her carefully against one of the blue exercise mats.

She sat up on her elbows to watch what he was doing. She was rewarded greatly. His muscles moved as he finished removing his shorts, and boxer briefs. His erection sprung free and she felt the slight panic, she wasn't a virgin but how would all of him fit?

Caine knelt between her thighs.

"I want to remove them with my teeth." Caine licked his full lips once more and Ava swore she was about to go into convulsions.

She was a bounty for his tongue. Caine could already taste her as if he had been there thousands of times before and he could not wait to go back each time. Her arousal flooded his senses. He crouched at first, kissing her lips chastely before making his way down her nude body. She was so soft and warm to his touch. Every hint of anger and annoyance was gone from her body, she was yielding to him and she was glorious. Caine kissed the supple flesh of her hips and moved lower. The banquet continued. Her taste was perfect to him. It matched her. There was even a spice about her that he could not place. His tongue dipped twice, licking the split of her lower lips, each time he pushed deeper. Her reactions were reward enough for him. Once he found her clitoris he sucked on it softly at first, but building for more intensity he held her still even though she bucked her hips and one of her long sculpted legs went around his shoulders, she pulled him closer.

Ava's body was his to command. His mouth was worshipping her and she had no objections, he lay out so he was eye to eye with his breathtaking prize. His tongue rolled and swirled her most sensitive flesh and she thrashed wildly. He gazed up her body and caught her stare. Her teeth cut hard into her lip she was watched him, her. The blood was building; he could see the stain of red. The fact that she was watching him cranked him up further. He dipped his head and buried his mouth once more.

He could play her body like a fiddle; he knew just when to bring on the pleasure and when to rest it. Caine was toying with her; he brought her to the golden edge over and over. His talented lips were relentless. She started to grind herself against his face and she wasn't the only one who earned pleasure from this movement. The moan she heard from him was music to her ears. Ava didn't know what this meant to either of them, she just concentrated on the intense pleasure she was being rewarded with.

"Caine. I'm going to explode," she warned him in a low whisper.

He didn't respond vocally, instead she felt one of his fingers sweep past her folds and into her core; she had to bite her lip to keep from screaming out. His hand moved with the same rhythm as his lips. Ava pulled her own hair and started to grind her hips over and over. She was taking her orgasm; she was intent on enjoying every single second of it.

The thought of her orgasm must have been pleasurable to him because he would not stop. Ava's toes curled and her moans became more pronounced as Caine continued. Her core tightened like a vice around his fingers, but somehow he kept going. He found the perfect spot and Ava's body detonated. There was no stopping the rush of pleasure that hit her hard. She screamed and began to breathe heavier. Her legs began to shake.

"CAINE!" Her panted call of his name was loud and in the middle of her body's release.

He lifted his head and licked his glistening lips clean. Caine kissed his way back up her body. No words were exchanged, but the cocky attitude he had did not need anything added. She could read his smirk. His lips dragged to hers, she could taste her juices on his lips. There was something erotic and naughty about the small movements of their mouths now, perhaps it was the fact she could taste herself.

Caine positioned himself between her legs and trailed his lips to her neck. "You are glorious when you cum for me."

He meant the words he spoke to her. Caine hoisted one of her legs back around his hip. His eyes still locked on Ava's, he could not look away from her beauty. She held his face between her soft hands and pressed soft kisses to his lips, chin, temples, and his neck. A fire lit within him. Caine wanted her every way he could have her. This could not be a mistake. Perhaps it could work? He ventured a thought further; maybe this demonic mating could last? He could not see himself ever getting bored of the way she felt wrapped around him.

Slowly, tortuously slow he pressed into her. He felt her body open and accept him inch by inch.

"You have to have at least one more for me right now." He pressed a kiss to her forehead, then another to her lips.

Her mouth jumped to life once more and their lips tangled quickly, and after that their tongues added to the tango. Once he was buried in her to the hilt he paused, he wanted nothing but her pleasure and he let her body adjust to his girth before slowly withdrawing from her almost completely then pushing himself back in. He kept the beat slow for a while, her core was wet, and soon she was pumping her hips to meet his again.

Soon he picked up his pace, his body met hers over and over. He kept speeding up until they were both panting, her hips continued to thrust to meet his. His Ava could be quite greedy when it came to lusty pleasures. His body was thrusting and claiming her. He felt the need to own her in every way he possibly could. Their scents were combining in the air and he rumbled deep in his chest, the sound of his approval increased with each meeting of their bodies. All control was gone for both of them.

"Please don't stop," her tone begged him more than her words. If she wanted more he was willing to oblige.

"Anything you want," he assured her.

His lips crashed against hers again. Her body tightened around him once more. It was not a surprise when she whimpered that she was going to cum for him again. Then it happened. The world paused when she came undone in his arms and around his cock. She quivered and held onto him as if he were the anchor keeping her on earth. She moaned his name over and over again in her guttural voice. With the scent of her pleasure in the air he continued to pump into her, her own fluids the perfect lubricant for him. Soon his balls tightened and he felt himself spill into her core, he barked a curse as he came for her.

Caine collapsed on top of her, they both panted from the explosive sex they just had. He rolled onto his side next to her, his strong arms wrapped around her and tucked her into his side.

"I hope I didn't cross the line." His fingertips traced her collarbone.

"No, you didn't." Her fingers were feeling the muscles of his arms, learning him.

"What do you have planned for the evening?" he asked, slightly protective for new reasons.

"I work a mid shift, then, I think I am going to relax in the bath tub.".

"Mind if I join you?" He picked up easily.

"Only if you rub my shoulders and feet," she stipulated.

"Your wish is my command."

"Then, you may." She smirked at him.

"Good. I must venture to the pit today. Happy Halloween to us." He checked his watch and sprung up.

"Who lit the fire under your ass?" Ava stared at him.

"I have a standing appointment I am going to be late for if I do not go." He leaned down and kissed her face.

"See you later, I guess?" Her voice was almost wounded.

"Try and stop me from coming to you, my vixen," he annunciated the word "my" to make her feel more confident of the appeal she held for him.

Ava returned home swiftly. She smelled like Caine. She could swear her pores were filled with him. The way he controlled her body was incredible. She relished every kiss, touch, and moment they shared at the facility. When she looked at her clock, she realized she was running late. She smirked. The shimmering power would come in handy for Halloween, after all.

The change in the air was becoming easier to sense and control. Ava shimmered into the alley behind her work, where she normally parked her car. When she arrived Ava noticed Tonya was already there. Ava's job was to relieve her, handle the side work, and then she would have to clean and go home. It was a short shift since it was time for midterms. Her boss always took consideration for college schedules. .

Caine regretted his appointment with Avaraz kept him from soaking up Ava's post-coital bliss. She was radiant. Had he become addicted to her so fast? Her taste was... he couldn't explain it. There were no words that good enough to describe her. She was his demon. She was his. He shocked himself with the urge to claim her. Would she want to be claimed? Why was he behaving like such a pussy? Caine shook his head. His hair, still damp from sex, flopped in his face. Hell. He smelled like her. It would be a sin to him to wash away her scent. Caine was, however, more concerned with his meeting. He was going to smell like Ava and sex when he met with Avaraz.

The closer he got to the wall where Avaraz was held the harder he concentrated on his own mental blocks to keep Avaraz out. Even though he was chained to the wall, and much of his energy was absorbed, he was still very powerful, especially in the mind. Avaraz could break any walls down. Caine just hoped he could hide his secret for this visit. It was never fun to talk about your sexual conquests, but this was Avaraz's daughter.

Avaraz heard Caine's approach. He was full of turmoil, and he was hiding something that Avaraz could not discern from the distance that remained between them. When Caine was close enough, he had his mental barriers up stronger than ever before. This was abnormal for their visits.

"What troubles you, my friend?" Avaraz's age showed.

"Nothing, Avaraz," Caine answered too quickly. This led to Avaraz pressing his will silently.

He softly went into Caine's head, slipping past the guards easily. Demons were easiest for Avaraz to read, especially when he knew them as well as he knew Caine. The recent memories were what he was attempting to hide. Avaraz entered them and what he saw brought anger to his heart, and nearly brought tears to his eyes.

"How dare you?" Avaraz pulled against the chains wishing he could strangle Caine with them.

"What?" Caine was shocked.

"I did not send you to Ava to seduce her! I sent you to protect her. How could you fuck my daughter?" Avaraz snarled.

While Caine was in hell, Ava took the opportunity to practice small tricks against Tonya using her powers. Small bursts of electricity hit Tonya when she used the registers. Ava could barely contain her giggles. She was enjoying her brief time with Tonya for a change. The rest of Ava's shift dragged on. When Dom finally came out to tell her it was time to count down, Ava almost ran to the back room to close out. She hurried through the count and returned with her deposit in hand.

"See you next week," Dom said casually as he went back behind the bar.

"What?"

"You have the rest of the week off to study for your mid-terms." He sounded almost as dumbfounded as Ava.

"Oh, yeah." She laughed at herself. She couldn't believe it was Halloween already and she had been in school for weeks already.

"How about I give you a kiss for good luck?" he asked with his most charming smile.

"Thanks, but I'm kind of seeing someone," she explained and looked at her hands.

"Oh," he sounded almost mournful at that, "I get it, all good. A prize like you can't be single for long." He winked.

"Thanks, Dom. You're still an amazing guy." She winked and went out the door quickly before things could get more awkward.

CHAPTER 8

Ava filled the bathtub and soaked her sore muscles. Caine knew exactly what to do to her body to bring her immense pleasure. It was a mind blowing sexual experience. Ava rested her eyes and began to drift into a gentle sleep.

The images began to dance in her head. First, she saw her normal little kitchen. She hears the doorbell chime, but when she answers it, her demonic powers take over and she strikes down four children in the middle of their chorus of trick or treats. Ava flew into a sitting position. She felt the power stirring in her hand. It felt so real. Sobs to wreaked havoc on her body. Her fingers pulled for the plug. She quickly dried off, dressed, and went to make tea. She could not get over how real the scene felt.

An image came into Ava's mind once more. The scene before her played out in a matter of moments. There was another knock at the door. This time, her power broke through the door, annihilating the frame and the children behind it. She screamed out and won her mind back. There was someone or something in her mind. Ava tried pushing her blocks out and it failed. Whoever it was had a deep grip of her mind. She continued the fight as best she could. When she finally was able to control her voice, her scream echoed off the walls. She was screaming for Caine, but he didn't come.

The screams soon turned silent, pleading. Each vision was worse than the last. Ava could feel her eyes change from their violet hue to pure undiluted red. With the color change, came more power. The electricity was still in her repertoire of weapons, but the newest one she gained access to was fire. Another vision bombarded her senses. This time, she opened the door and launched fireballs at what she saw. The screams of the children horrified her and churned her stomach.

As soon as the vision finished and she had temporary control of her body, she ran to her bedroom and locked herself away. She rocked back and forth, mumbling her prayer for help, her prayer for Caine. She did not understand who was doing this to her, or why. Then, there was silence. She did not feel any itching, or prodding in her mind. She had control of herself once more.

Suddenly, the visions returned worse than ever. She felt the hellfire on her arm. Another round of torture commenced. The clawing in her mind intensified. She begged the demon, or whatever it was, to show and stop what it was doing to her.

She lost herself to the tears.

Meanwhile, the argument between the two males raged on. Avaraz was still on the offensive about his daughter being taken to bed by another demon. He did not want her damned to the same life he had lived for so long.

"You went into my mind?"

"Yes, because you were untruthful!" He was still pulling, causing himself to weaken.

"I did not know how to tell you," Caine offered his pitiful answer.

"I did not send you to watch my daughter undress and spill your seed within her!" Avaraz was still pissed.

"I did not intend that either, my friend," Caine began.

"You have lost the privilege of calling yourself my friend. You are a traitor. My daughter is not some whore to add to your conquests!" he yelled the words.

"She is not just a conquest." Caine's voice was small.

"What?" Avaraz sputtered.

"She's not just a conquest. I want her." Caine sounded so sure of himself.

"What makes you think I will let you have my daughter?" Avaraz's glare penetrated deep into Caine's mind, and soul.

Caine remained silent and appeared to contemplate his reply

Anger still coursed through him. "I cannot believe the gall you have. You fucked my daughter." Avaraz's voice was one of the deepest anger, confusion, and accusation.

"I have to go." Caine shimmered out the moment he heard Ava's screams of panic and pain.

"Perhaps my friend could change for her." Avaraz closed his eyes and concentrated on the Caine's future.

When Caine shimmered into the room Ava was in, his heart broke for her. The sounds coming from her were devastating. He walked forward and grabbed her arm gently.

"Ava, Ava look at me." He tried to keep his own panic at bay.

She screamed at him, "GET AWAY! YOU'RE NOT REAL!"

"Ava, open your eyes." He tilted her chin so she was forced to look at him.

Her eyes opened slightly, as if she expected to be hit if she opened them much wider. "Caine!" He could feel the relief come from her body.

"Ava, what's wrong?" He held her out slightly so he could look at her face. He brushed her hair back to get a good look at her.

"I was seeing things. I watched myself killing kids!" She sobbed and fell onto his chest.

He held her close and rubbed her back. Someone was playing with her mind, and Caine wanted to kill the bastard for hurting her. Again, his protective side surprised him. Her agony was becoming more and more palpable to him. The only thing he could do was to continue his feeble attempts to comfort her.

"Ava, calm yourself and tell me exactly what happened," he urged.

She took several sobbing breaths before she could speak. "I felt someone in my head. It was like they were scraping my brain, and I couldn't stop them. They made me see different versions of myself hurting kids."

Caine had no idea what he could say to make the situation any better, so he opted for silence. In Caine's experience, you could always say so much more by saying nothing at all. It was something he learned through his many years of being a demon. Yet he was still learning something new daily, such as his attachment to another demon that became so strong extremely fast. He continued to rub her back.

"I can't hurt children," she murmured after a while. The sadness struck Caine deeply.

"You don't have to. We target people who already have a window into their soul for us to use. We emphasize what is already there," his voice was just as small as hers.

Ava appreciated the silence they were allowing themselves. She was still trying to sort through what happened. The feeling of the power in her hand was enticing, seductive even. The pain she felt at even potentially hurting children was something she could not endure. Caine's presence was comforting to her, even if she couldn't vocalize how much he helped. She prayed he knew what she felt.

"Who did that?" she asked.

"I don't know. There are many who can, to be honest. Some hunters can, too. With how real it felt to you, I believe it could have been someone that was from an upper level." His hand went through her hair.

"Why would an upper level demon want to hurt me? I'm a demon, too." Her brows creased.

"Some want to have more power, some want more souls, and some just want chaos. Take your pick," his voice was bitter.

"Why, though? How many know about me?"

"Not many, I thought only your father and I knew about you." He rubbed his chin in thought. Who else could have known?

She remained silent after that, her own thoughts torturing her again.

"You need to work harder on protecting your mind. If you are half the seer your father is, you could be under almost constant attack. Seers hold the information to the future. Every faction in hell will want that and hunters will torture you to get it." Caine's voice rang with authority.

"How? How can I protect against something so vicious coming into my head?" Ava would do anything to never see that vision of her killing innocent children again.

"We will train you. I will go harder at your mind, and I will start to hurt you mentally. You will feel me in there, and you will have to learn to push me back out, no matter how hard I fight. If someone gets a hold of the information that will hurt you most, they will use it." He stopped rubbing her back and gazed into her eyes.

"I will do my best. I'll try," she whispered and rested her head on his shoulder, the warmth of his body comforting her more now that she knew what was expected in the near future.

"We can start tomorrow." He pressed his lips to hers. He could taste the remnant of fear on her.

"I am more than willing," a soft note of determination had entered her voice.

"That is what I like to hear." Caine picked up Ava and walked her to her bed.

With every ounce of gentleness he possessed, he laid her softly against her duvet. Once he was sure of her comfort, he moved to the opposite side of the bed and lay next to her. She put her hand on his chest to feel the flesh-coated muscle that had owned her earlier that day.

The weight of the day had finally begun to take its toll on Ava. Her eyes drifted closed, but she was battling back her sleep. She had Caine in her bed. She wanted to do so many things that would tire her further, but she settled for questions, since the day had been rough on them both.

"How old are you?" she asked.

"I am very old." He laughed.

"How many women have you had?" she asked, quoting one of her favorite movies.

"I am a demon of lust. I lost count ages ago." He sounded somewhat regretful.

"Was I any good?" She had to know.

"You were more than amazing." He tapped the tip of her nose gently.

She smiled; sleep trying to pull her further under. "Do you like me?"

Did she even have to question whether or not he liked her? He was falling in love with her, despite his best efforts to reject her. When this fiasco began, Caine wanted nothing more than to finish the request from a friend and go on about his business. But she, somehow, wormed her little ass into his heart. So much so, that he doubted he owned it anymore.

Caine watched Ava be slowly taken over by sleep. Every nuance of her face was entertaining to him. She was beautiful. Her breathing began to slow once she relaxed enough. He stared. The epiphany of feeling more for her than he ever did for anyone else was taking over. He could not believe what he felt. It was strange. He went from being a demon warrior who took pleasure in the flesh, and pleasure in the kill, to a sap. Truth be told, he couldn't be happier about it.

Once he was sure she was in deep enough slumber, he edged his arm out from under her head. He backed from the bed silently and took one more look at her before writing a note. With a quick flourish of his wrist, he finished the message and kissed her temple before turning off the lights to her room.

With one last look around, he shimmered to hell to continue his conversation with his oldest friend.

Caine returned with a flash of light. Determination in every inch of his body, he stalked forward with renewed purpose. He was going to do what he never imagined he would.

"Yes, I did have sex with your daughter, Avaraz, but I think I want her as my mate."

Avaraz stopped his yelling. His eyes softened slightly. "You know how rare a true mating is? Are you sure it is not just withdrawal from lack of sex?" He growled.

"I know. I can't explain it. When I was with her, I felt complete. There was a piece of me that I had been missing. I think I was content and happy." Caine rambled slightly.

"Will you protect her?" Avaraz asked.

"Till my dying breath" he answered immediately.

"No hesitation, you must be sure or a fool," the older demon answered.

"Perhaps, I am both. I do love your daughter, and that love has made me a fool to some things," Caine answered quickly again.

"Will she be happy with you?" Avaraz's concern grew.

"Aye, I believe she will be."

"Does she love you as much as you love her?" The question was one of deep contemplation for the both of them.

"I have been inside her mind. I believe she does, yes. I cannot be one hundred percent sure, because she has not admitted her total adoration of me, yet." Caine half-smiled.

"If she will have you, then I will accept your request for my daughter." Avaraz nodded. He had a lot of time to think since he was bound to the wall.

"Thank you, my friend." Caine bowed his head.

"I still have one more favor to ask," Avaraz noted.

"Anything, I will do and give anything."

"I will not ask it of you right now. I will when the time is right. Go to my daughter. Be merry. There are plenty of obstacles in the future. Enjoy the moment." Avaraz nodded and closed his eyes.

"Thank you again." Caine shimmered out of the pit quickly to return to Ava.

The result of his visit to hell was surprising. Caine was unsure what changed Avaraz's mind about Ava and his relationship progressing. When he arrived in Ava's bedroom, she was still resting. Good, she needed it after the trauma she went through.

Caine thought back on his own childhood after he climbed back into bed with Ava. He had grown up fighting, battling, and doing every unspeakable act he could think of, and that would earn him praise. He grew up knowing his demon nature. She hadn't, but she had come so far. She did need his protection for now, though. Silently, he vowed she would have it.

His arms snaked around her midsection and he joined her in a restful sleep.

The next morning, Ava woke up first. Caine was tangled with her, all tension gone from his face. She savored the moment before she maneuvered out of bed carefully, so she didn't wake him up. She padded to the kitchen in her robe to make tea.

"Surprise, my princess," a voice sounded behind her.

Ava froze and turned to face the source. "Uncle!"

"Yes, my little one. How have you been?" he asked, concern marring his features.

"I have been well. When did you get in?" she fibbed a little, but she wanted to hear of her uncle's trip.

"I just got home. I hope you will give me leave. I need to unpack and will talk to you later of my trip." He spoke like a diplomat.

"Okay, Uncle, I have to do training in a bit, so I will see you later today," she reminded him gently of her demon training.

"Yes, of course. Where is the bastard?" He cocked his head to the side.

"Caine? He is not a bastard. He is actually a good guy, and he is around." Ava did not want her uncle to know that Caine spent the night, and they had gone much further than he could anticipate.

"Whatever you say, child." Isaac kissed her forehead lovingly. "I will see you later." He started toward his room without another word.

Ava breathed a sigh of relief when she was alone again. She made herself tea and sat at the counter, waiting for Caine to come find her. She felt relief when his strong arms wrapped around her.

"Good morning, beautiful," he rumbled in her ear.

"Good morning." She shuddered softly. The sound of his sexy voice made her lower body quiver.

"I am glad to see I affect you." He gave her a cocky grin.

"I bet you are." She gave him a knowing look.

"Did you make breakfast?" He looked shocked.

"Yeah, I made bacon, biscuits, toast, eggs, and I had fruit salad left over." She shrugged.

"No one has cooked for me before." He stared at the small spread.

"Have you ever stuck around for breakfast?" Ava grinned and joked about his past. Shame crossed his face.

"No, but I believe that has changed," he admitted.

"I am glad you think it has."

"Well, I am going to eat. You go get your fine ass ready and we'll get you to training." She felt his eyes roam over her body as he spoke

"All right, all right." She stood up from the table to get dressed.

Caine held onto Ava's hip while they shimmered into his makeshift training facility. The familiar scent of sweat and stale air hit his nostrils hard. It was familiar. The newest scent that came to them was Ava. Ava's pleasure had taken over him. The scent of her arousal lingered. He was glad he didn't leave a window open. He smirked.

"I smell you," he noted aloud.

"Really?" She sniffed her hair.

"That's not what I mean." He licked his lips with promise.

"Let's just get to work." She blushed and knocked his shoulder playfully.

He pulled her toward the mats. "You got it. We have to work on your ability to keep people out more. The invasion cannot be repeated. The further you come into our world, the more you will know, and the more valuable the information will be."

"I got it." She braced herself.

"I am going to start low again today to remind you what to do, but I will get to full power this time. I will not take it easy on you. You need the practice." He licked his teeth.

"I said I got it," she said once more.

"Protect your memory of what we did on this mat." He grinned seductively, which caused her to flush even deeper.

"Bring it on, demon." She joked.

With those final words, the games began. At first, Ava let him enter her mind easily. She wanted him to feel how she felt when he took her on the mat. Each caress meant so much to her, and it was her way of letting him know how intense it was.

Then, things got serious. He added a slight amount of mental pain when she joked too much. She fought back. Each time it became easier. Caine began to grasp onto her mind. She fought to get him out. Her growls echoed through the training area over and over again. The mental prodding began to get truly painful. Ava pushed harder. Her desperation made it easier. Her desire to protect the precious memories of Caine overrode her other senses. Her exhaustion gave way to a new determination.

After several hours of practice, Caine felt more confident in her abilities to protect her mind. He pulled Ava onto his lap after they finished.

"I saw your father today," he said casually.

"You did?" she squeaked.

"Yes, he could smell you on me." When Caine spoke Ava flushed scarlet.

"WHAT?" She blinked.

"Needless to say, he knows what happened." Caine chuckled at her reaction.

"What did he say?" She questioned.

"Not much. He was pretty mad at me, at first. Then, something changed his mind." He shrugged.

"Oh…" she trailed off.

"How about you go home, relax in a bath and I will be by shortly," Caine offered.

"That is very seductive of you." She chuckled and his heart warmed.

"I just have a few errands to run. Perhaps, I'll join you?" he suggested.

"Perfect. Now, get going." She kissed him and quickly shimmered out before he could respond.

He chuckled. "She's getting more and more like me every day."

Caine disappeared himself. This time he was going to find her a proper bouquet of roses to confess that she owned him.

Yes, yes, a little half-breed whipped Caine the lothario demon.

From the moment she got home, Ava had a foreboding feeling of what was coming, but she shrugged it off as her nerves once more. She did as Caine suggested, and the moment her body sunk into the steaming water, she groaned audibly. The mental exertion took a lot out of her. The muscles that she had to lock into place were sore. She felt as if she had run a marathon with no training. Her eyes closed and she banished the memory of what happened after her last bath. The steam cleared her senses and she soon lost the ominous feeling she arrived home with.

"Mmm, Caine, show yourself," she murmured when she felt a gentle push at the corner of her consciousness.

There was no audible reply. There was another push on her mind. Ava sat up. "Caine, this isn't funny. Show yourself." Her voice was sterner the second time.

The push got deeper, harder, and more intense. Ava's stomach curled and went into her throat. She stood from her bath and reached for her robe, before she planted her feet and shoved whoever was in her mind out.

This time it lasted. She had peace in her mind. To be safe, she called for Caine.

Hellfire swooped up the creature that had been attempting to gather information. He was being summoned to his master. The process was painless normally, but the anger his master kept within made the process horrific to experience. The smoke swirled around him while he waited for his master's instructions.

"Is the girl a threat to us?" he asked, his ghastly voice barely above a whisper.

"She is the demon, Avaraz's, daughter. She is getting stronger by the day. I have kept tabs on her master." The imp cast his eyes to the floor.

A mighty roar came from his master.

"Show me what you saw," he demanded.

The lower level imp came to his master and gave his hand over. Immediately, the master pierced his thoughts and searched through everything. When he was done, the master's strong backhand came against his face.

"This will never do," he growled the words, "I need you to go kill the girl this time. No playing with her. Just kill her."

"Yes, master," he tried not to stutter the words.

"Get out of my sight." The master waved his hand and smoke surrounded him again.

Within an instant, he was back in the world he had come to know. He had to kill the half-breed demon when Caine wasn't around. How would he do this?

Ava waited for Caine in her oversized bed. The pinging in her head had stopped and she finally had silence. Her uncle was at the shop for the night. He was doing inventory on the new items he had acquired on his trip. She didn't realize how tired she truly was. Once her head hit the pillow, she fell into a deep sleep.

What felt like hours later, Ava woke up and found she was still alone. When her feet hit the floor, she shuddered from the cold that attacked her soles. She wiggled into her favorite pair of athletic pants and a sweatshirt from her school. She reached for her slippers and slid them on before she started her walk down to the kitchen.

She figured Caine was in hell, or some sort of demon business took over his evening. Ava's lower lip protruded. She was pouting over what stole him away from her. After she pranced down to the kitchen, she started to cook herself a snack. The stove began to heat when she flipped the dial on, and she set the pan on it. Her hands worked on coating a piece of chicken breast to fry it.

There was a knock at her door and Ava took off, padding toward the rapping knocks to answer it. She had no clue what was waiting for her. Perhaps it was the mailman? No, it was into the night, and they were usually done a lot earlier. Maybe it was a delivery for her uncle? Another negative, he had his deliveries sent to the store. When she reached the door and there was more knocks, she assumed it was Caine playing some sort of joke, or respecting her space and pretending to be human and knocking. Yeah, right. That was not Caine's style.

CHAPTER 9

Ava's hand went for the ornate door handle. It was cool to her touch. As an afterthought Ava looked through the peephole, she saw nothing outside her door. On the off chance it was an actual package, Ava opened the door and looked for a brown box. She saw nothing. There was a shimmer of magic behind her. She turned and spoke at the same time.

"Caine, that isn't funny. You don't have to play human." She laughed, but when she completed the turn, she stopped.

It wasn't Caine. There was nobody behind her. Confusion colored her face. Perhaps she was mistaken, or her imagination was playing tricks just like when she was a child. She closed the door and flipped the lock into place then went back to the kitchen.

When she rounded the corner into the kitchen, she saw someone in the middle of the room. This had to be what she felt in the hallway moments before. Ava stood her ground. Whoever it was had donned a hood and stood silent before her.

"Who are you?" her voice shook.

Deafening silence greeted her still.

"You need to get out of here before I call the cops." Ava threatened.

That is when the person made a lightening fast movement. He launched a fireball at her. She dove out of the direct path, and the fireball hit the wall right behind where she had been standing and singed a hole straight through to the hallway.

"*SHOW YOURSELF!*" she demanded.

There was a maniacal laugh from under the hood. A bony hand came up and pulled back the hood. Ava gasped.

"Michael?" She was genuinely confused.

"Hello, my love," his voice was full of venom.

Another fireball launched from the hand, which had once tried to caress her. Ava went spiraling into the hallway. It was an emergency situation. Michael was a demon. How did she never pick up on it? She took off up the stairs with Michael following behind her. The sound of his boots hitting the hardwood was the soundtrack to her terror.

Ava went for her room. She tried to gather herself in the mere seconds allowed her. She could feel the panic to contact Caine fire off her emergency need.

Michael was getting closer and closer. The only option she had was to fight or take flight. Whatever sort of demon he was, Ava knew one thing for sure. He was higher ranking than her. She did not possess the battle skills that he had. There was scraping at her bedroom door. He was toying with her. Then, it sounded like a battering ram was being repeatedly slammed into the door.

The scent of a burning fire tingled Ava's nose. Michael was throwing fireballs at her door to break his way in. This was nothing but a game to him. His voice was frantic and sounded like he had lost touch with reality.

"Ava, you should have joined with me. You could have lived," he whispered.

"Go to hell," was her swift response.

"Been there, done that. I live there, bitch." He threw back. The door was beginning to splinter apart.

She ventured a swift glance and Michael's usually kind eyes were bright and demented. They were blood red and looked the part of a full-breed demon assassin. He was crazed. There was more crashing against her door. She didn't want her uncle to come home and risk his safety. Ava had to plan this perfectly.

When the door finally gave way, Ava waited until Michael wound up his arm to throw another fireball at her. She countered with her own ball. The electricity flowed fast and powerful from her hand, and connected with his chest. Michael flew backwards and she was surprised at the strength of her attack. When he recovered and was standing to attack her again, she took the moment and concentrated hard on an escape route. Then, she shimmered out.

In an attempt to find safety, Ava shimmered to the one place Caine told her that demons could not track easily.

Killing the girl would prove more difficult than he imagined. He started by playing cat and mouse. She must have seen too many scary movies. Instead of running outside where he might have had some hesitation about using his powers in front of the humans, the simple girl ran to her bedroom. He chuckled darkly as he pursued her.

When he got to her room, he continued the terrible mind fuck. He barraged the door with his fireballs. The sound was deafening. Each crackle from the fire was music to his ears, as were her uneasy breaths. He finally busted through and she had an offensive attack ready for him. It was a genuine surprise. He was going to enjoy dismembering her, limb by sexy limb. His master would approve of his brutality on this matter.

Then she shimmered out.

Michael walked silently to where she had just shimmered from and placed his hand up. He could feel the magic that remained next to him. His eyes closed momentarily, and he picked up exactly where she went. What a tricky little girl. She shimmered into the graveyard where her mother was buried. He grinned.

"Let the game continue, little demon." He quickly gathered his senses and shimmered.

The graveyard was frigid. When Ava's feet touched the ground, she immediately wished she'd had the foresight to put on shoes before she left, or at least grab them. There was not much time. She knew that the intruder she once called her friend was following her. She took off running. The heavy fog was coming in. An eerie feeling settled into the cemetery. Ava willed it to get heavier. Her footsteps were silent as she began to move faster and faster. Then, she heard a demonic laugh echo through the tombstones.

"Come out, little bitch." He yelled for her.

She remained silent. She could make it impossible, or at least harder to find her, and give Caine time to catch up and come to her aid against the more powerful demon. Her limbs pumped harder and harder to make her move away from her enemy, but the bass in his voice echoed, and it sounded as if he were coming from every direction.

Ava ran and ran until she could find some bearing in the large cemetery. She whipped her head around when she saw the tree she grew up playing around. Her uncle would bring her to visit the graves, and she found solace there. She strengthened the shields in her mind and went toward the looming tree. It looked ominous in the distance, but once there, she would be able to find where she was desperate to hide.

Caine had told Ava that demons could not track exactly where a demon was on hallowed ground, but they could sense their presence. She could feel Michael, but that was it at the moment. The beating of her heart was thunderous, but she kept running. Another sharp inhale caused her to feel the stinging of the cold air. Her mahogany hair whipped in every direction as she looked around to check that she was still safe. She wasn't paying attention and her foot caught on something. When she pulled her leg up to her chest to check it, there was some blood, but no bones sticking from the skin. She got up with a slight glance toward the marker. It was Peter's; Peter Keznik's grave. Ava's eyes widened. She got up and started to limp. She knew Michael was closing in on her. His power was becoming easier to read in the wind.

Before he could close in any further, Ava limped into the mausoleum. Unlike her dream from before, she wasn't joined by the sound of her father's voice. She curled in on herself, hiding in a corner behind the central decorative podium. Michael's footfalls become obvious. She could tell he was attempting to rouse her from her hiding spot. At random intervals, she would hear headstones breaking, and fireballs hitting the collections of private tombs.

Silence greeted her once again. Michael must have moved away. She couldn't feel his power anymore. Ava stood and started to open the door of the mausoleum just a crack to feel the air, and found nothing. Her shoulder pressed into the door and there was a soft groan from the metal of the door when she opened it. She stopped and waited. Again, there was nothing to suggest he was still there. Perhaps he thought she had shimmered out since he couldn't follow.

The moment she took a deep breath, she tasted something in the air. It was pure rage and soured on her tongue. Ava took another soft step out of her hiding spot. There was still only silence in the air until she felt something crashing down on top of her. The weight took her down onto her back. She hit the ground hard. Her head snapped back, and her vision went blurry for a minute. When it finally cleared, she saw Michael on top of her. Her arms were pinned to her chest and he was straddling her hips to keep her legs still.

"There you are, beautiful." He leaned in and shuddered when he inhaled her.

"Get off me," she growled.

"No, your scent is positively beautiful when you are fearful." He ground himself into her pants.

She could only glare.

"You see, you should have come with me instead of aligning with Caine. There is an uprising coming. There will soon be demon against demon wars." He laughed.

"What?" She struggled. She figured if he talked, she could get information out of him.

"You could have been on my side, with my kind, and you would have been protected. Look, Caine is a demon of lust, and he leaves you all the time so he can go fuck real women and be satisfied doing things you can never do." He played on her insecurities.

"Fuck you!" she spat in his face.

"If you had fucked me, you might have lived." A knife materialized in his hand and he started to cut open her shirt.

She struggled harder.

"You see, your fear calls to me. It makes me fucking hard. It calls to him too, undoubtedly. He has been near you. I've smelled his scent all over you for weeks. I was sent to acquire you, or kill you, but killing you is quickly becoming the answer."

"You're wrong." She tried to buy more time as she eyed the large bowie knife that he now held.

"You are, sweetheart. He left you here, knowing that you don't know what you need to know for protection, and he still hasn't come to your aid." The knife bit into the flesh of her neck. Michael hissed, "You smell divine."

She continued to thrash about against his hold.

"Keep still or this will be over faster than I want." He brandished the knife in front of her eyes then dragged the tip along the side of her face.

He dug the point in just a little more around her neck. She fought the urge to cry out and give him any satisfaction. The silver blade pushed into her chest, he yanked open her shirt and gazed at her breasts.

"It is a shame you are going to go to waste. A lust demon always is beautifully endowed with talents." He leaned his mouth down and captured the blood that trickled from her neck and chest with his snakelike tongue.

She screamed loudly. The thrashing from her body grew. She knew she would die. She just hoped it would be fast and that the torture would not be great.

"It won't be." He laughed at her.

She pegged him with another glare. His mouth came back down to hers. When his tongue slipped into her mouth once more, she bit down as hard as she could. Michael reared back, howling in pain. Blood surrounded his mouth.

Ava spit out a large amount of blood and wiped her lips on her blouse. Michael's hands came back down with all the force he could possibly possess. His eyes glowed with unadulterated hatred.

"That will cost you, bitch," he growled the words, "I will have to teach you a lesson." Blood flew from his mouth with his venomous words, the demonic healing factor barely having time to kick in yet.

His hand went between them as he reached for his fly. He struggled with getting the metal zipper to release him. Her struggles became more pronounced, and it seemed to fuel his depravity.

"I wonder if you will scream." His top lip lifted into a snarl.

His one hand began to wander further down her curves. Ava concentrated hard. She couldn't push him off, and his extreme grip on her wrist prevented her from shimmering away from him. The only avenue she had left was to use her energy against him. She swallowed hard and closed her eyes, so she couldn't see what he was doing. She felt another cut from his knife slice into her. This time, it was in her stomach. Instead of sputtering out in pain, Ava fought back. She collected the power from her anger and forced it through her body. The energy built quickly and ran over her body.

She heard him cry out in pain once more. A sadistic smile lit her face. His pain was good for her. When she wiggled her arm from his grasp, she launched another energy ball at him. The large and powerful ball hit his stomach and sent him onto his back. She scrambled to get away, her feet moving just as fast as before.

She ventured a look behind, her but he had disappeared. She stopped and began to call for Caine once more, when she was bashed in the head with something. She fell to the ground and blackness took over.

Michael had crushed a piece of rubble from a headstone into the side of Ava's head. He smirked at what he had done after her body was crumpled on the ground. It was too simple. He used his feet to roll her onto her back then crouched over her, cracking his neck. He felt the master's influence coursing through him. The master was brutal in what he wanted done to the young half-breed. Michael leaned down and pressed his lips to her passed out mouth. He met no resistance. She was out cold. It would be easy to do anything he wanted.

The thought angered him. If Caine hadn't come to her aid, he would have been able to seduce her to his side. Caine ruined the plan. She fucked Caine, but she never considered having sex with *him*. More anger came pouring into him. Michael opened his hand and his palm met the side of her face. He repeated the action till she stirred.

Ava woke to pain. Something was slapping her. Awareness slowly came back to her. It was Michael, and he was pissed off about her. The demonic side of her reared up in defense. She opened her eyes and she could feel they had changed. The pupils dilated and were pure red. They were no longer the violet they usually were. Ava began her struggles anew, pushing him away.

He sat up and his eyes glowed down at her. He licked his lips and locked his gaze with hers.

"Good morning, sleeping beauty," he sneered.

There was barely time for her to give a venomous reply, when Michael flew off of her body against his will. The shock on Michael's face was evidence of that. She heard several tombstones being crushed by the weight of Michael's body being sent through them. Ava looked in the direction the power had come from, and Caine was running toward them at full speed. Caine's massive body was hulking even at the distance that was still between them. He was pissed and there was no mistaking the anger that rolled from him in thick waves. She knew he was going to tear Michael limb from limb.

Caine stopped for a moment, his eyes softened slightly as they roamed over Ava, and his red eyes burned with intensity and sorrow. All hell was going to break loose. Ava felt the side of her face throb, as Caine did his inventory of her body.

Caine roared with unmitigated hatred. When he saw the other male on top of his female, the protective male instinct came out. The fact Ava was hurt made the feelings worse. He could smell her blood in the air. The burst of power came from within. The primal desire to protect a true mate was paramount.

When he saw Michael's body fly, he felt a slight satisfaction. He stopped to check on Ava.

"Are you okay?" He felt queasy as he assessed her up close.

"Yeah," she hissed through her teeth in an attempt to hide her pain.

"No, you're not," he growled.

"Obviously. Don't ask stupid questions." She attempted to sit up.

"Don't. I'm going to fucking kill that prick, finally. Then, I'll take you home." Caine's rough voice softened slightly.

Before Ava could reply, there was a blast of hellfire that licked around Caine's entire body. Michael was back up, and it seemed he grew three times his size with his anger. He was running right for Caine.

Caine braced himself for the collision. Michael was a demon, and a physically strong one at that. They locked arms. It was a battle of wills. They moved, each trying to overpower, throw, and trip the other. Michael flexed his muscles and attempted to push Caine further. In the blink of an eye, Caine returned the force and kicked Michael's knee. He heard the other demon's leg snap at the contact, and then came the cry of anguish.

His smile spread when he heard the pain he inflicted on Michael. Caine decided to taunt him. He had to distract the other demon and trick him into making a mistake.

"How does it feel to know I've been inside her?" He baited.

"Fuck you," Michael spat.

"No, I fucked her. She moaned so nicely for me, too." His voice was smooth and sultry.

A growl was the only reply.

"She whimpered my name as she came. Over and over again, she came apart in my arms."

The growl continued and Michael's arm wobbled slightly as anger shook him.

"I never tasted a woman so sweet, till I was between her legs, lapping at her juices," Caine continued.

That was the final straw. Michael's obsession transcended the job, and was the root of who he had become. Caine wondered how many times he'd attempted to turn Ava to whatever faction he came from. The male's eyes were lit up like blood-red Christmas lights. He was glowing with his rage.

Caine used his own anger and tossed him aside. Michael was quick, however, to get back up and start another round. He threw ball after ball of hellfire at Caine, who quickly blocked them all. Only the slightest singe frayed at the ends of his leather bracelets. Caine shimmered behind him and launched his own offensive strikes. The pure energy that came from him was in a long, continuous bolt. His teeth showed from the effort.

The use of power in such a manner took from both the male demons. Caine tripped over a grave and

Michael used the loss of footing against him and fired at his legs. It was Caine's turn to spiral.

When the crack of Caine's skull echoed through the air, Michael felt vindicated. Blood once again permeated the air around him. That was when he remembered the girl he had once attempted to convert. The half-breed, Ava, could have been a good trophy for him to boast of around the pits. She chose to go with Caine and his band of bastardized demons. The master could have earned her respect. He turned to find her and continue his punishment. She would beg for death before he would relent and give it to her.

Nothing. Where had she gone? Did she run? Caine's great love left him alone to fight a demon. The woman he fucked, and used against Michael, had run at the first sign of trouble. If that wasn't a normal female, Michael didn't know what was. He had to chuckle. He walked to the spot where she had last been seen and let his tongue snake out to taste her energy. She hadn't shimmered right there. She ran. Michael followed the trail for a moment.

"Come out, come out, wherever you are," he taunted.

A bolt of electricity slammed into his side. Michael turned and fired in the direction of the bolts. He waited for her cry of agony, but heard nothing. He started to walk toward it, but was hit from behind.

"Ava, you are doing nothing but buying yourself more agony before I kill you, and further pissing me off," he yelled at the half-breed

She was a crafty little girl. She shimmered several times before she would attack. The difficulty of tracking on hallowed ground was tenfold over what it was elsewhere. He waited, learned the pattern of the music. When she stopped for a single moment, Michael launched another fireball.

There was a tiny whimper coming from the direction of his attack. He followed the voice. There was fresh blood from Ava on the ground.

"Did I hurt you, baby? Just think of how much more pain is coming your insolent little way," he threatened.

There was silence again and Michael could feel the shimmers happening slower.

"I do not have to kill you, beautiful. If you join me I can convince them to spare you." He let that hang in the air and stilled his movements while he searched for her.

He always maintained a "Plan B" for harder kills.

Ava was hit. The hellfire burned into her flesh. She couldn't contain her gasp when it went through her. She swore the pain was worse than anything she experienced before. Michael was stalking her movements. She shimmered until her energy faded to the point of no return then she took off running to Caine's side.

"Caine... Caine, wake up!" She shook his side and whispered urgently into his ear.

There was no response from him. He was bleeding profusely, so she picked up his head and cradled it in her lap. Her fingers ran through his thick hair. She whispered her will for him to be healed. She called him back to consciousness. She kissed his head, but there was no change in him.

Without warning, Ava's hair was fisted and pulled up. She dropped Caine's head and screamed loudly as she was dragged to her feet.

"You are beginning to really piss me off," Michael's voice was sickly sweet in her ear.

"Fuck off," she fired.

"In due time. You owe me a pound of flesh, which I will exact before I torture and kill you, little demon." He inhaled.

Ava struggled against his hold again.

"Go ahead. Keep fighting. It makes you smell marvelous," Michael noted.

In her defiance, Ava stopped immediately. She squared her shoulders the best she could and attempted to run the current once more. Her energy was depleted but she had to try.

"If you would have just relented, I could have convinced my master to take you in, even if you are a filthy half-breed who doesn't even know her true potential," He mused aloud.

"How about you fight me and kill me like a warrior, instead of trying to bore me to death?" Ava spoke up finally.

"You disrespectful little bitch. If you want to fight, we will fight, but that will not make your death any faster" He shook her as if she was a bobble-head toy, but then he released her and pushed her away.

"Let's get this over with." Ava gulped. She knew she could not take on a pure-bred demon, let alone one that had been alive for God knew how long.

Michael chuckled and without another warning of their dance of death, he began to rapid-fire his fireballs at her. Ava dove into a roll to avoid getting hit by the first round. He continued his assault until he hit her square in the stomach. She slowed down, and he approached.

"The funny thing about being a mortal. You don't come back from something like this." Michael was enjoying himself.

Ava couldn't form a coherent sentence. She grunted from the pain that was her companion. It was the only thing that let her know this wasn't some nightmare. Everything slowed down. It felt surreal.

"Who is your master?" she muttered.

"Do I look so stupid? No matter how close you are to your ultimate goal, you never give away the ending. Has television taught you anything or have you been too stupid as a mortal to absorb anything that isn't screamed at you by some stiff in a suit?" he ranted.

Silence greeted Michael. Ava was biding her time and conserving her energy.

"This is only going to hurt a lot. I am going to strip your soul, Ava."

Worry flooded her. Caine had explained in detail about removing a soul from a demon. It was painful, and the demon would forever be shamed. It was the beginning of an eternity of pain. The demon would never be allowed to rest. She could not outrun him. He froze Ava in place. She knew prayers from a demon would carry little, but as her uncle had taught her, she prayed in her time of need.

Her mind worked fast. She prayed that her uncle would be safe, that he would be left alone and not burdened with her death. Ava's hopes went to Caine; that he would live and his soul would not be stripped, as well. She prayed that her friends would not be targeted. If they smelled like demon, a demon hunter could attack them. She also prayed that she had the strength to carry out her next act.

Michael's mind wasn't protected. He believed he had already won. Ava slipped in easily. She began to try and take control of his extremities. First, she stopped his legs from coming any closer to her.

"What the fuck?" he snarled and she felt the fight over his limbs begin.

He attempted to forcibly remove her from his mind, but as she learned from her own torture, she held on, her hold was sticking into his pain receptors as if she were digging nails directly into his brain. Her mind bit into his and began to cause him pain. She focused hard on the center of his mind, forcing more and more pain into him. Each ounce of pain she had felt, she returned to him tenfold.

They stood there, in silence, and in the battle for supremacy of his body. She had nothing to lose and that made her a dangerous foe. She would fight tooth and nail to live and she was backed into a corner. The fog between them became heavier as the magic swirled and hung in the air. Ava gritted her teeth as she exerted herself further.

He was surprised the half-breed bitch was such a worthy adversary. Where Caine had neglected her training in certain aspects, he had made up for it with her mental game. Michael stood in silence while he fought for his body. Her mind was strong and hung on for dear life inside his head. She must have known what he had in store for her, and when he got free she was going to pay dearly. He could already taste her salty tears streaming down her face.

Michael played the scene in the back of his head. He hoped she would see his depravity and lose her focus long enough for him to force her out so that he could take command of her body. It would have been so much sweeter to make her prepare herself for his taking. Ava stayed still. She didn't even blink. If she saw what he was thinking, she gave away nothing. He had to admit, her poker face was strong.

Without warning, Michael felt another intruder. Caine swiftly wrapped his arms around Michael and pulled him into a chokehold he could not escape.

Caine's physical strength had rejuvenated in a brief time.

"Now, you'll be her bitch." Caine taunted once again.

Ava walked closer and closer. Her mind still locked with Michael's as they struggled within. The hellfire in her eyes was unmistakable. She was bent on revenge.

"Can you really take someone's life, Ava? You are human, and that makes you weak." He glared at her as he played on her human half.

"You aren't worthy to even breathe. I'm doing your master a favor by getting rid of your sniveling, annoying, ass-kissing, bullshit." Ava was almost close enough to touch.

Caine's grip tightened with each step Ava took. It would be so easy to strike her down. She was within swinging distance. Michael struggled for freedom; freedom of his body and freedom of his mind.

"What shall we do with him, Ava?" Caine asked.

"I think dismembering him would be a good start. Of course, afterwards we need to burn him." Ava was thorough.

"Or you could pump me for information and then let me go for an exchange." Michael was a survivor first, which often was synonymous with coward.

He launched a sudden attack on Ava's mind. She was composed, cool; oddly cool. It was as if she had been in training for a mental attack a lot longer than she had known. Then, it hit him. Michael had forgotten she was the half-breed daughter of Avaraz. She, of course, would have more mental powers.

"Do you want your father out of prison?" He asked.

"Stop trying to prolong your death. It is only wasting time and pissing me off," She toyed with him, just as he had with her.

Ava's eyes were still violent red. She embraced her demon half completely. The once violet eyes he gazed into were gone. Michael smirked.

"Why are you so happy? You didn't win, Michael." Ava stood her ground, brave-faced.

"You are a demon. You cannot stay in the mortal realm." Michael chuckled.

"You don't get to stay alive," she fired back.

"I may lose my life, but you've lost yours, as well. You get to live to miss yours, though." Michael laughed loudly. The madness had taken him.

Ava probed into Michael's mind and stopped the laughing quickly. The pain hit his system fast and his legs buckled.

"Enough of this playing. Goodbye, Michael." Ava came closer and Michael's head lolled forward.

She gripped each side of his face and looked into the eyes of a demented demon that had lost the battle. With no more warning, Ava planted her feet, and called upon her father for strength. She plunged her fist into Michael's chest in a swift movement. His final sound was a gasp. Ava held the heart of another being in her hand.

Caine felt no more resistance in the corpse after Ava removed Michael's heart. She surprised him by the vicious show. She remained calm. Ava now stood in silence, almost marveling at the heart she held. Caine wanted to be thorough, and show Ava that she was not a monster. He threw a small ball of hellfire at the ground. When it stayed, he returned to the body and pulled the head off of Michael's body. Caine casually began to move pieces of the corpse into the fire to burn, so he could not be resurrected.

"Ava?" Caine turned to look at her.

There was no answer. She stood in a shocked silence.

"You did not have a choice. He had to die," Caine reminded her.

She turned to face him, her face pale. She dropped the bloody heart and held her midriff. The scent of her blood hit his nose. She was still hurt. Ava's face was devoid of color as she looked at him, and then she collapsed onto the ground in front of him.

CHAPTER 10

Caine's heart lurched in his chest when he saw Ava begin to fade. Her blank stare was unlike her. He blamed himself when her head hit the icy ground hard. Caine had heard the thud from the distance. She had to have been exhausted. Caine stepped away from the burning body of Michael. There were many questions that had to be answered for that. He would get to the bottom of it eventually. The more important matter of Ava's safety was at hand.

He went to her side without another moment of hesitation and wrapped his arms around her. She made no noise. Caine pressed his head against her chest and heard the steady thrumming of her heart. That comforted him. She was alive. His arms tightened as he ran through the scenarios that could have played out. Caine was lucky. Whoever was standing behind

Michael and his attack had to have been powerful. The unbidden thought came to his mind, even though Caine's priority was Ava, something had changed within him. Perhaps, that was how it would stay.

Caine shimmered to Ava's home. When he appeared in the kitchen, Isaac jumped to his feet and began to berate Caine and yell at Ava.

"Isaac, if you do not quiet yourself, I will cut off your vocal cords for the night," Caine growled.

"What?" Isaac stammered.

"Ava is okay. She is just exhausted, and if you wake her up you will have me to deal with," Caine warned.

"What happened?" Isaac hissed

"She fought a demon," he stated simply and began to walk toward her bedroom.

Isaac shoved back from the table and followed swiftly. "She fought one of your demons? She is one of you! How can you attack your own?" he growled.

"Back off, Isaac, it wasn't one of mine. He was from another faction." Caine spun on his heels to look Isaac in the face, while he gave him the information.

Caine continued back up the stairs to get Ava into her bed. Once she was comfortably resting, he took a moment to look at the soft contours of her face. Pulling the sheet over her, he brushed the hair gently from her face. It was damp from the sweat of her exertion. His lips caressed her forehead then he left the room as quietly as he could.

When he exited the door, he immediately ran into Isaac, who had been watching. He was seething from the tender display Caine had just shown to Ava.

"Shall we go to the kitchen before you begin spewing?" Caine walked past Ava's caretaker.

"What you have done is grossly inappropriate!" Isaac immediately started in a hushed tone.

"What I have done?" Caine was angered.

"Yes, you have pursued my niece without regard to what you said, or what you said were your feelings were toward her."

"I know what I told you at the beginning was probably the only reason you allowed me near her, you are protective of her and I understand why. Isaac, I didn't mean to fall in love with her. It happened and I could not stop myself, believe me when I say that I tried." Caine rubbed over his face.

"You love her?" Isaac's features were covered in shocked.

"Yes, I do. I want her, and I don't want others to touch her." His admission seemed to quell some of the anger from Isaac, but not all of it.

"If you love her, then why are you damning her to a life in hell?" Isaac protested.

"I am not damning her. I showed her who she is. She took to it well. Isaac, she gave herself to me willingly." No father figure would want to hear that.

The puce color returned to Isaac's face. "You had sex with her? You are nothing but a lying demon!" Isaac growled his words now.

"I only slept with her after I realized how in love with her I was, and spare me the talk. I already had it with Avaraz," Caine dismissed Isaac's anger.

"You will listen to what I have to say, demon. I cared for her. I changed her diapers when she was a baby. I protected her, I bled for her, and I loved her from the day she was born. When she cried herself to sleep, *I* was there. Her first love, her first heartbreak, her first everything, I was there. Not you. You don't come in now and pretend you know better because you're a demon and she's a half-breed. You're a demon, while she's only half. She still has human nature and tendencies. You will never dismiss me as being more of a father to her than that Avaraz joke. She is my daughter more than his." Isaac surprised Caine with his rant. The mortal stood up to him, earning his respect.

Caine held his tongue while Isaac spoke. By the end of his rant, the old man was nearly yelling. "Now, Isaac, I told you to be quiet," Caine barked loudly and forced a strong wind to push Isaac into his chair, and then Caine sat across from him.

"If you think each day has not pained my friend, Avaraz, knowing someone killed the only woman he loved, and the daughter he made with her would never know him, you are sadly mistaken." Caine's glare narrowed on the man.

"Then, where is this great friend of yours? Surely, a demon as fierce as he, could break any enchantment," Isaac insulted the demon who had taught him so much. Caine flexed his hand.

Just as Caine was going to fire off his own round of insults, he heard a feminine throat clearing from the doorway.

"Ava, you're awake." Caine stood and crossed to her, his arm snaking around her hips.

When Ava rested, she had dreams of her father again. He was smiling at her. It was oddly confusing. She woke easily after he whispered soft words of encouragement into her ear. Ava was oddly refreshed when she came to. She heard muffled voices through the floorboards.

She sat up to listen. It was Uncle and Caine.

Oh, no, they were discussing her personal life. Her face met her palm quickly. She decided to make her way down the stairs so she could save her uncle from the over-shares that Caine would definitely not spare him from. Then, she heard it. The bomb of them sleeping together hit Isaac's ears and Ava paused. Her gallant uncle's voice began to rise as he spoke of his love for her. She was touched. He did consider himself her father, just as she did too. She, however, still wanted to meet Avaraz. He was her birth father.

She rounded the corner into the kitchen and cleared her throat. The arguing stopped. The frown she was wearing lifted when Caine came to her and felt the need to touch her. Ava leaned into his touch.

"Uncle, I am so happy to see you are safe." She beamed at him. His eyes were on the spots where Ava was touching Caine.

"My niece, you seem to have been busy lately." The tone wasn't accusatory, just surprised.

"Yes, I have, Uncle. I have learned so much by Caine's side." Her smile radiated from within.

"I see you are quite happy with yourself," Isaac noted.

"I am. I do want your permission for one more thing, though." Ava was going to go no matter what she just wanted his approval.

"What is that, my niece?" His eyes were on her eyes, watching her like a hawk, as he had done for many years. He needed a break.

"I want to meet my father." She looked down.

Caine pulled his arms away and held her at length.

"Ava, you don't know what you're asking for," Caine warned her.

"I don't care. I want to meet him. I need to." She batted her eyes at him.

"Ava, listen to him. You do not belong there," Isaac chimed in.

"I want to meet him. Either you support it, or you don't. How do you know I don't belong there? I am a half-breed demon, Uncle Isaac, I may be able to find answers there. I will get many answers from Avaraz," she ended the conversation.

Caine and Isaac both uttered curse words of different natures.

"I heard those," Ava joked.

"I wasn't trying to hide mine." Caine held his head in his hand, worry coloring his features.

She sighed. Isaac remained silent in his contemplation.

"Ava, your father does not wish for you to go to Hell," Caine warned.

"So?" Her tone was full of petulance. "I think I have earned the goddamned right to meet him after all these years. If you're afraid of him, you can tell him I overpowered you and forced you to take me." She crossed her arms over her chest.

"I'll take you, but there's no way in hell that I will say you overpowered me," Caine scoffed.

She slid her hand into his and winked. Ava had won. She knew it. The way she pranced said all it needed to for Caine. He rolled his eyes at her.

"Hold on tight, princess." He grabbed her around her hips and shimmered with a tight hold on her into the pits.

"Stay safe, my niece," Isaac finally whispered.

Ava coughed at first. The air was stale and dry. She looked over at Caine, who stood tall with a brow raised.

"You get used to it after a while." He shrugged.

"Does being a half-breed have anything to do with it?" she had to ask.

"Maybe, there aren't many half breeds in the world. We're not exactly encouraged to mate with humans, and the offspring is usually killed pretty quickly, if there is any. It's a weakness most of the time."

Caine led the way toward the wall where her father was kept. His eyes never left the path directly in front of them, but Ava's were the opposite. She had never been to hell. Even her dreams could not prepare her for such a place. It smelled of brimstone and what she would imagine despair to smell like, if it had a real scent.

Her hand was squeezed tighter in Caine's when she started to slow from her desire to look around constantly. The audible groans of the damned sounded beyond the wall.

"It's depressing," she whispered.

"Yes, it is quite depressing. But again, darling, you get used to it."

"How much further is it?" she asked, still looking around.

"Not much. He may not be happy with me for this." Caine sounded like he wanted to turn back.

"You let me deal with him." She chuckled.

"Are you laughing at me?" He stopped and whipped around to face her.

Caine's physical strength had rejuvenated in a brief time.

"Now, you'll be her bitch." Caine taunted once again.

Ava walked closer and closer. Her mind still locked with Michael's as they struggled within. The hellfire in her eyes was unmistakable. She was bent on revenge.

"Can you really take someone's life, Ava? You are human, and that makes you weak." He glared at her as he played on her human half.

"You aren't worthy to even breathe. I'm doing your master a favor by getting rid of your sniveling, annoying, ass-kissing, bullshit." Ava was almost close enough to touch.

Caine's grip tightened with each step Ava took. It would be so easy to strike her down. She was within swinging distance. Michael struggled for freedom; freedom of his body and freedom of his mind.

"What shall we do with him, Ava?" Caine asked.

"I think dismembering him would be a good start. Of course, afterwards we need to burn him." Ava was thorough.

"Or you could pump me for information and then let me go for an exchange." Michael was a survivor first, which often was synonymous with coward.

He launched a sudden attack on Ava's mind. She was composed, cool; oddly cool. It was as if she had been in training for a mental attack a lot longer than she had known. Then, it hit him. Michael had forgotten she was the half-breed daughter of Avaraz. She, of course, would have more mental powers.

"Do you want your father out of prison?" He asked.

"Stop trying to prolong your death. It is only wasting time and pissing me off," She toyed with him, just as he had with her.

Ava's eyes were still violent red. She embraced her demon half completely. The once violet eyes he gazed into were gone. Michael smirked.

"Why are you so happy? You didn't win, Michael." Ava stood her ground, brave-faced.

"You are a demon. You cannot stay in the mortal realm." Michael chuckled.

"You don't get to stay alive," she fired back.

"I may lose my life, but you've lost yours, as well. You get to live to miss yours, though." Michael laughed loudly. The madness had taken him.

Ava probed into Michael's mind and stopped the laughing quickly. The pain hit his system fast and his legs buckled.

"Enough of this playing. Goodbye, Michael." Ava came closer and Michael's head lolled forward.

She gripped each side of his face and looked into the eyes of a demented demon that had lost the battle. With no more warning, Ava planted her feet, and called upon her father for strength. She plunged her fist into Michael's chest in a swift movement. His final sound was a gasp. Ava held the heart of another being in her hand.

"Maybe, what will happen if I am?" she challenged.

"You will see," he warned and continued down the path.

They walked in silence the rest of the way. When Ava opened her mouth to speak, he whirled around with his finger to his lips and shushed her. She laughed and stepped on the back of his leather shoe. When he turned on her again, she smirked and whispered, "Flat tire?"

He grumbled about her stepping on the back of his heel, as they approached where Avaraz was held. Caine nudged her forward gently. "Go see him."

"Aren't you coming with me?" she asked.

"No, you two need a moment alone." Caine relaxed against a portion of the wall.

"Okay…" Ava nervously walked toward the unexplored part of the wall.

There was silence, and then there were soft footfalls coming closer and closer. Avaraz listened intently. Who was coming for him? He recognized each of his very few visitors by the sound of their feet hitting the ground. This one was different, however, and the shield blocking him was strong. He would have to wait until he could catch the scent of his visitor.

The scent flowed from the feminine visitor. The warmth of her heart had yet to be tainted by all the evil of the world he lived in. It reminded him of his Christina. Christina. Panic settled into his stomach. Surely, Christina's soul was at peace? That was part of his penance deal. The steps were coming closer and closer. Soon, he would be able to see who it was. Caine would not have brought his Ava to the pit of sin, would he? No. Maybe? He did sleep with her and profess his love, after all, even to the woman's father.

When he saw Ava coming around the corner, his heart sank to the pit of his stomach. She was not supposed to be in Hell. He had seen the outcome many times before in his visions.

"Ava, what are you doing here?" He attempted to pull on the shackles again.

"I am here to visit you: father," she tried the word aloud. It sounded weird.

"Get out of here before you get caught." More worry.

"Not until we talk. You're my father. You owe me that much." She was stubborn, just like her mother.

"Fine," he relented.

"Did you love my mom?" she had to ask.

"Yes, with every fiber of my being. I believe she was my true mate." His eyes glassed over.

"You believe she was, even after all of this?" She motioned to his shackles.

"Yes, even more so now. After seeing horrible things, she was still my beacon of hope. She was still

208

the only being I ever loved more than myself." He nodded in his assessment.

"How do you know she was the right one?" she asked.

"When it is right, something inside you says it is, and you just know my daughter." He smiled at his words.

"Do you love me?" she again had to ask. Avaraz wished it would be the end of her questions.

"With every breath I took, since I learned of your existence, I have loved you. You and your mother are what kept me alive this long." He tried to reach to her hand.

"Did you ever try to come to me?"

"Every dream you had of me was me trying to reach you. I have known and loved you, Ava. You are my daughter, and you may not know me well, but I know you." He smiled weakly at her.

"Why are you attached to the wall?" she asked.

"I refused to kill your mom and you." Avaraz sounded angry.

"Why did you have to kill us?"

"They said you could join our faction or die. I offered a third option and they accepted."

"I want you freed." She straightened her spine.

"I will serve my punishment, Ava. You will not interfere." He attempted to use a fatherly voice against her.

"They wanted me in the faction. I am choosing my life. I want to be in the faction. I want to free you, Avaraz." She sounded firm.

"Is this because of Caine, as well?" Avaraz looked at his daughter.

"Part of it is, yes. Part of it, also, is that I finally know who I am."

"Let me protect you. You will never escape this." He warned his daughter.

"Listen, I am a grown woman, and I can choose my fate. If it means having the person I love in my life, knowing whom I am, and knowing my father, I will be a demon. It is in my blood. Let me choose how I want to live. If the elders will take the trade, that is."

Caine had to settle himself before he turned the corner. Ava wanted a life with him even if it meant being a demon, and being involved in the pit. Would she still feel that way even if they had to hunt down and find out for whom Michael worked? Would she still feel that way when she was away from her uncle for months at a time, and possibly longer, to protect him? Humans were not meant for their world. Would she leave her uncle behind in order to save his life?

"Ava, do you know what you are saying?" Avaraz asked. Caine continued to walk closer.

"Yes, I do." She sounded confident.

"Are you sure?" Caine asked.

"Yes," she said.

"You are too stubborn, my child." Avaraz chuckled.

"Yes," She sighed, "Caine, I want to see the elders."

"Are you sure?" Caine asked.

"Will you please stop asking that? I am sure!" She was getting angry.

"Caine, no!" Avaraz shouted.

He was confused. On the one hand, he wanted to honor the oath he took, pledging to Avaraz to protect his daughter from such monstrosities she would encounter in the demon world. On the other, selfish, hand, he wanted her in the faction, so he could keep a hold on her, and never be without her. Caine hesitated.

"Caine. Please. I want my father freed." There was heartbreak in her voice, so he gave in. Caine summoned the demons.

"I will call them, Ava," he relented.

"NO!" Avaraz shouted and pulled his restraints.

"I have to. I need to know you, and if I know you're here being hurt, I couldn't live with myself," she confessed.

The men were silenced by the arrival of the elders of the faction.

"Why were we summoned?" the tallest of the three asked.

"I want to make a deal." Ava spoke up.

The debate began. Ava had to speak above her father's objections time after time. He was angry. He begged her to change her mind, and begged the faction leaders to deny her request. She would not be swayed. Once she made up her mind, it was a firm decision. She was stubborn, just like her mother. The elders scheduled the marking ceremony immediately.

The three demons walked Ava and Caine to the temple where the elders resided. Caine gripped Ava's hand to support her. Her fear of the unknown could be tasted in the air. Once the door was closed, the hellfire rose by the altar. The marking would be permanent, and she would never be able to hide or destroy it. The hellfire magic was something she could never change.

Caine whispered the details of the marking into her ear. It was fairly simple. They would ask if she was sure, they would burn her, and then give her a chalice to drink from. The drink had no meaning outside of ceremony. They all gathered into a semi-circle around the altar, with Ava directly in front of it.

"Where would you like your mark, child?" the female asked again.

"Where can I have it?" she asked and Caine's eyes bulged.

"You can have it on your wrist, or your ass," the large one spoke out with a dark growl.

Caine's growl made them all turn.

"I guess my left wrist." She held up her arm.

The growl from Caine subsided quickly. "Good, I don't want *OTHERS* to see you nude." The warning went without saying.

The small woman chuckled.

"Let's get this going," Ava changed the subject as she looked at the glyph at the end of the fire poker.

The symbol for lust was staring at her. She watched the poker heat further. The graphite colored metal changed to an almost yellow-orange. Ava's eyebrows jumped up and she gulped.

"It is time, young one. Are you sure you wish to continue?" the diminutive one asked.

"Yes, I am sure." She wanted her father to be free.

"I hereby command you unto our will for our race, and for the demonic faction you were born into." The words were followed by a brief pause.

Seconds seemed to pass slowly. Ava was waiting for what felt like hours for the burn to come. The female picked up the poker and slowly walked toward her. Ava looked at Caine. There was a mixture of pity and pride in them. Pity for the pain she was going to endure, and pride that she chose this path. Without another warning, or even a word, Ava felt the metal press into her wrist. Her eyes tore off of Caine and went straight to the site of the heat.

A scream bubbled up before Ava could stop it. The pain was intense. She could feel it sear through all of her veins, from the top of her head to the bottom of her feet. Her scream subsided as she grew accustomed to the pain. The hellfire spread fast. The metal was removed, and there was a slight lag in Ava's body.

"It is done. Welcome to our ranks," the largest said again.

"Thank you. Now, for my father," she insisted.

"Yes, your father." He snapped his fingers.

"Where is he?" She wanted to rub her wrist, but it was so raw from the burn. The scent of burned flesh loomed in the air.

"He is by the wall, still. The chains are off and he can move about freely. If he disobeys our orders once more, though, it will be death for him, not imprisonment," he warned.

"I understand, and I am sure he does, too," she reassured him.

"You may go now," the three said in unison.

Caine took Ava's right hand and led her out the door. They started back toward the wall. He was pulling her alongside him.

"No going back now. You belong to us." He chuckled.

She laughed with him. The immediate danger to her life was gone. At least, she thought it was. Her father had been freed from his prison, and she was marked for her future now. It made sense. The eyes, the dreams, the accidental things that happened when she was sad or angry, they all made sense to her. She was a demon.

Avaraz was slumped by his spot on the wall. There were no magical shackles around his limbs and neck any longer. He was free to live, as was she. For the first time since she entered hell, she took a deep breath. It was becoming normal finally. She kneeled by her father's beaten body.

"Father." She gently placed her hand on his shoulder.

"Ava, please say you did not join us," he pleaded one last time.

"No, I gave my word so I could be with you and Caine." She held his face to look at hers.

"Why? We wanted more for you?" Avaraz sounded full of the deepest sorrow a father could feel.

"I feel like this is where I belong, father. The demonic half of me never fully fit in, and I would rather be here and learn about the half I felt I had lost than be ignorant to what I am. Please, accept it." She pressed the back of his hand to her cheek.

The contact seemed to help him. He brought his eyes to hers.

"You gave up your freedom for mine," he said, the pang of guilt deep within him.

"No, long ago, you gave up yours for mine, so I could choose." She wrapped her arms around him.

Avaraz winced slightly at the contact at first, and then it was like a live wire bit him. He came to his senses. He realized he was holding his daughter and the energy flowed into him swiftly. The many nights he spent imagining what she would feel like in his arms were nothing compared to the pure joy that overcame him when he held his daughter for the first time, so many years later.

"Ava, I am so sorry." He was apologizing for a lifetime of regrets he harbored.

"The past is the past. We just need to move forward," she suggested, being terribly reasonable.

"I can't believe you are here," e answered.

"I am." She began to choke up and released his hug.

"We should go," Caine interrupted.

"Why?" she asked. She didn't want to leave her father yet.

"All of us should go. We have business to tend to." He smirked.

"Okay…"

"With Isaac," Caine announced.

"Oh." A look of worry crossed her face.

"I would like to talk to Isaac," Avaraz spoke up again.

"I guess we are going, then." She mashed her lip between her teeth, like her mother always did when she was nervous.

Isaac waited for what felt like an eternity, until the air shimmered behind him. He whirled around to see Ava, standing with two male demons. One was Caine. The other was the one who condemned his sister to death by mating with her.

"You son of a bitch." Isaac launched at the demon, and to his credit, the demon didn't move. He accepted the punch to the jaw without a noise.

"Uncle!" Ava grabbed his arm before he could wind up for another attack.

"That is the demon who killed your mother!" he snarled.

"No, he didn't. He loved mom. Just stop for a minute. Please," she begged.

He did not wish to upset Ava, so although hatred was the only emotion he could access, he calmed down and straightened his clothing. Isaac reached for his niece's hand and pulled her into a hug.

"I have been worried about you, *MY* girl," he whispered loud enough for the others to hear.

"I am fine, better than fine, really," she assured him.

"You joined the demons, then?" he asked.

"Yes, I wanted to free Avaraz." Her eyes were soft. She was so tenderhearted.

"What does this mean for you, though?" He asked.

"It means I am a half-breed demon who is going to be part of a faction. I know who I am, now." She added.

"Will you be residing in hell?" His brows creased in deep worry.

"No, she does not have to," Caine spoke up.

Ava and Isaac both looked at him, and he smiled. "I guess I don't have to," she added.

"Good," Isaac noted.

"There is a catch, though. In order to protect you, she won't be able to live here. There is a rogue demon, or faction, loose that we have to find. If they used your mind, or used you against Ava, they could crumble her," Caine told them.

"I see." Isaac sounded sorrowful.

The three men looked at Ava when they heard her soft sob inhale.

"Are you well, my niece?" Isaac asked.

"Yes, I'm fine," she brushed it off.

She walked outside at that. The older demon followed her, leaving Caine and Isaac to discuss Ava's future.

Avaraz followed Ava outside. She was not hiding, but she was not going to attempt small talk if she did not feel she could.

"I know it is hard to leave those you love, Ava. It is the hardest thing you will ever do. You will think of him daily. I can promise you that much." He stopped when she pegged him with her violet gaze.

"If you are trying to make me feel better, you really need to work on your people skills," she snapped.

"I am being honest, Ava. You need to do this or you put his life at risk. He would be killed swiftly if you had regular contact with him. There are hunters, and now this new threat. Would you rather see him, or know he is safe?" Avaraz asked.

"I understand, but that doesn't make it easier to leave." Her eyes clouded fast. The tears fell, and Avaraz sat next to her.

"It'll be okay, Ava." He rubbed her shoulders and let her cry. The conversation halted

Caine smiled at his conquest. "Thank you, Isaac. Your opinion in this matter does mean very much."

"Yes, but if any mistakes are made, I don't care who you are or what your powers are; I will come for vengeance against you," Isaac warned the demon.

"Yes, I understand, and will do my best not to make the worst mistake of my life. I will pack up her necessities. This will always be her home." Caine offered.

"You will not touch her private belongings. She will pack herself. She is a big girl." Isaac did not want Caine looking at Ava's undergarments. The scoundrel would have enjoyed it too much.

When Ava came back into the house, she looked around. It was one of the last times she would be there for a while. The emotional toll was increasing.

"Ava, come to me," her uncle spoke from her bedroom.

She went without another word and found him sitting on her bed, the photo album of her mother's pictures and letters she had written for him and Ava in hand. Ava loved having at least a small part of her mother in the letters. She kept them safe in the album. It looked like Isaac had more to add. His sister had written many letters for different events in Ava's life, he was now going to give them to her to read in her own time.

"Are you okay, Uncle?" She sat next to him.

"Yes, I am fine. I am more worried for you. I know you must go. I accept it, and will not make it harder for you. I want you to know I love you, even if you are a demon. Your mother made a decision, and so did you. You are a stubborn woman just like she was, and I cannot keep you away from what you want and love." He patted her leg and handed her the photo album before he walked out of the room, leaving her alone to pack her clothes.

Once she was done, she gazed around her room. She had packed a few of her favorite things from the walls that she cherished deeply then went downstairs to join the men who were all sitting around the kitchen table drinking coffee. Avaraz's eye was purpled and bruised from Isaac's attack earlier.

"I'm ready." She spoke and they all jumped up.

Isaac was the first to greet her. He pressed his lips to her forehead. "I will love you always, and you are always welcome here when you can."

"I know. I love you, too," She was choking up again.

"We better go. I called in a protection spell favor I am owed." Caine rubbed Ava's back openly in front of each man who was her father, biological and emotional.

"I will see you soon, Uncle." she said, emotion lacing her voice.

"I love you, Ava. Be safe. Caine, remember your promise," Isaac spoke.

With those last words from her uncle, Ava shimmered out of the house she grew up in. She didn't know what was ahead of her, but she at least knew she had Avaraz and Caine by her side.

Caine was waiting for Ava to follow his shimmer. The demons truly did have their finger in every business. The penthouse in the center of New York City cost a pretty penny. It overlooked Central Park and was spacious. There were wings to the penthouse. Avaraz was going to his own section, and Caine was going to share his with Ava. The words Isaac spoke to him resounded in his head, time after time. This was not something he could take lightly.

When Ava finally showed, he smiled. This was *his* female. Her eyes bulged at how incredible the view was. She walked to the window and looked out.

"He may be close, but I feel so far away," she whispered.

Caine's arms wrapped around her in an attempt to comfort her from the misery she felt. He gulped. "It will get easier with time. I have something for you," he followed up.

"A present?" she asked.

"Yes. Give me your wrist and close your eyes." The childlike excitement was plain for all to see.

"Okay," she placated him and stuck out her wrist.

His fingers made quick work, clasping something around it. When Ava opened her eyes, she saw leather straps, with a small silver heart dangling around them.

"Caine, it's beautiful." She marveled at the delicate woven straps around her wrist.

"I made it for you. Do you like it?" He nodded toward the new jewelry.

"I love it." She leaned into his chest for a kiss.

"I want you to know you have stolen my heart, little woman. Will you be my mate?" He asked.

"Yes." She said without hesitation.

"Good, because I couldn't live knowing someone else had you in their arms." He tightened his grasp around her and picked her up.

"What are you doing?" She giggled.

"I am going to remind you of why you agreed so fast to be mine." He chuckled and palmed her ass.

She knew danger was lurking close by. The brush with Michael had proven there were so many obstacles still to overcome. Ava pushed the thought of dangers away from her mind. She was in the arms of the man she had come to love so fast. The worry could wait for another day. That night was one to celebrate that she was alive and able to love. He whisked her into the bedroom and a night of a thousand pleasures began.

THE END

FOR NOW...

ABOUT THE AUTHOR

Lauren is a Tacoma, Washington native who has always enjoyed the art of writing. She lives with her loving husband, son, and two dogs. She is an avid reader of many genres. Lauren is currently attending school to enhance her writing ability. She looks forward to bringing more books and characters to life.

KEEP UP WITH LAUREN

On the Web: LaurenPeyton.com
On Twitter: Twitter.com/TheLaurenPeyton
On Facebook: Facebook.com/AuthorLaurenPeyton